Cherry
Whytock

Honeysuckle Lovelace

Ghosthunters

PICCADILLY PRESS · LONDON

For Grant and fluffy memories of Celeste.

First published in Great Britain in 2007
by Piccadilly Press Ltd,
5 Castle Road, London NW1 8PR
www.piccadillypress.co.uk

A catalogue record for this book is available from the British Library

ISBN: 978 1 85340 911 0 (trade paperback)

1 3 5 7 9 10 8 6 4 2

Printed and bound in Great Britain by Bookmarque Ltd
Cover design by Simon Davis
Cover illustration by Cherry Whytock
Typeset by Textype, Cambridge

Set in 12 Adobe Caslon

Chapter One

The Patchwork Snail sighed in the freezing canal as Honeysuckle Lovelace peered out from under the warm covers of her tiny bunk. It was still pitch black but Honeysuckle knew it had to be morning; she could hear her mum, Rita, clattering around in the world's smallest bathroom next door.

'Why can't this blooming houseboat have a proper bathroom?' Rita screeched. 'There's barely room to breathe in here, let alone have a proper bath . . .' There was a crash. '. . . and now I've dropped the blooming soap!'

Cranky! thought Honeysuckle to herself as she reached out and switched on the string of fairy lights that festooned the headboard of her bed. The lights made little dancing shadows across the ceiling and lit up dots of colour on the brightly painted walls of her cabin. She looked over the side of her bunk at the red furry slippers that Rita had bought her the week before during one of her charity shop trawls. She thought about climbing out and pushing her toes into their lovely, soft fluffiness but then she decided to stay exactly where she was. She would wait until Rita had finished in the 'ice cream tub' bath and had stuck on her fresh nicotine patches. Giving up smoking was Rita's greatest battle; that and trying to keep The Patchwork Snail afloat.

Honeysuckle lay back on her lacy pillow and pulled the bed covers up under her chin. She couldn't help smiling to herself. It was the first day of the Christmas holidays and the Dog Walkers' Club already had some bookings. Later that day she, Jaime, Anita and Billy were to take Mrs Whitely-Grub's poodle, Cupid, out for a walk. Blossom the bloodhound was coming too, along with Hamlet the Yorkshire terrier and Pudding, who was a sort of basset hound gone a bit wrong.

Mrs Whitely-Grub was the reason the Dog Walkers' Club had begun in the first place. She was one of Rita's clients at her hairdressing salon Curl Up and Dye. Mrs Whitely-Grub couldn't bear to think that Cupid might be unhappy left on his own while she had her blue rinse retouched, so she had always brought him with her to the salon. This made Rita hopping mad because she said the little pinkie-white poodle made smells and ate other people's chocolate biscuits, quite apart from getting in her way and yapping all the time.

Seeing Cupid sitting on his personal leopard-print cushion on one of her mum's pink salon chairs had given Honeysuckle her Brilliant Idea – to form a Dog Walkers' Club. At least that's what Honeysuckle told her mum, but truthfully there had been the sign in the tea-leaves as well.

Honeysuckle knew that she had special talents and reading tea-leaves was one of them. She was absolutely, positively and completely certain that she had fortune-telling powers. Her dad, Lenny, who had 'forgotten the way home' according to Rita before Honeysuckle even had a chance to remember him, had real Romany blood. Not only had he left her with a crystal ball, but Honeysuckle was also sure that she had inherited special gifts from him. Rita wasn't at all keen to be reminded of Lenny so Honeysuckle had kept her fortune-telling talents to herself and her friends.

'Yoo hoo, Honeybunch!' Rita trilled from the galley kitchen. 'Nearly time to shake a leg!'

She must have got the patches on now, thought Honeysuckle, as she snuggled further into her bunk. She was remembering how she had first seen the picture of a dog in her tea-leaves, the morning of her Brilliant Idea. And how forming the Dog Walkers' Club had led to an amazing investigation into The Case of Mrs Whitely-Grub and the Murdered Major. Except that wasn't quite what had happened and it had all been sorted out in the end. But that was when the police officer in charge of the case had met Rita. If he hadn't met Rita, they would never have started going out together . . .

'I'm making hot buttered toast!' Rita called before launching into a rousing chorus of 'Thank You For The Music'. That was too much for Honeysuckle: the smell of scrumptious toast *and* an Abba song were quite enough to coax her out of her snug cocoon. She joined in with the chorus while she wrapped her rainbow-striped blanket round her shoulders and popped her feet into her slippers.

'There you are!' said Rita beaming, as Honeysuckle shuffled into the minute galley kitchen of The Patchwork Snail. 'I've made you hot choccy,' she said, handing Honeysuckle a steaming rose-printed mug, 'with whipped cream on top as a special treat!'

Honeysuckle took the mug and wrapped her fingers round its comforting heat. She licked a blob of cream off the top and grinned at her mum. She loved it when Rita had time to have breakfast with her before going off to work, especially if, like today, Rita turned out to be in a good mood. She had already stoked up the little wood-burning stove so that the saloon glowed with warmth. The flickering flames made the beads of the countless necklaces that Rita had hung across the windows sparkle and gleam. Through the beads, Honeysuckle could see a thin glimmer of morning light reflecting in the icy darkness of the canal. She cuddled down into one of the velvet cushions on the long seat in the saloon and sipped her hot chocolate.

Rita, meanwhile, was trying to decide what to wear on her feet, while drinking her coffee and eating her breakfast. She had a slice of toast in her mouth and her mug in the one hand and was balancing precariously on the very high, spiky heel of a giraffe-print ankle boot.

'Mmmmph?' she grunted at Honeysuckle, who shook her head. She didn't really think that giraffe-print boots would go with the purple and black ribbed tights, shiny black pedal pushers and shocking pink fluffy jumper that her mum already had on. Besides, Rita's hair was

5

sort of black and white stripes at the moment (she had agreed to let her assistant, Nev, colour it for her because he said he would die of boredom if he didn't get to do something interesting soon) and Honeysuckle thought that with her mum's diamante chandelier-style earrings, it might all be a bit much.

'These then?' asked Rita, munching the crust of her toast and putting on a pair of plain, black biker boots.

'Much better,' said Honeysuckle, considering the boots. 'They're a bit like the ones Sergeant Monmouth wears—' She stopped short. Honeysuckle didn't want to discuss Sergeant Monmouth, especially not this early in the morning.

'Hmm. I suppose they are,' said Rita with a little smile. She fastened the final buckle on her left boot without meeting Honeysuckle's eye.

Seeing the boots made Honeysuckle remember some of the creepy crimes that Sergeant Monmouth insisted on describing whenever he was on The Patchwork Snail. There had been all that stuff he told them last night about bodies being fished out of the canal years years ago. It had given her the wobblies.

'I think the Sergeant might pop round this evening,' said Rita, running her hands through her hair. She always called him the Sergeant even though she knew perfectly well that his name was Derek. It was like a little private joke that she and Sergeant Monmouth had together and it made Honeysuckle feel quite queasy.

Rita hung the giraffe-print boots up by their heels on the rail above the window along with lots of her other shoes. This was one of her many space-saving ideas.

Honeysuckle was about to complain about the number of times the Sergeant came round when Rita said, 'Listen, Honeybunch, I must dash – I've got a million and one perms to do today!' She swooped down and gave Honeysuckle a lipsticky kiss while one of her huge earrings brushed the side of Honeysuckle's cheek. 'Have a gorgeous day. Good luck with the dog walking!' Rita pulled on her fake fur coat and hurtled through the boat and up the steps that rose from near the end of Honeysuckle's bunk. 'Be sure to leave everything shipshape,' she said as she banged open the hatch.

A blast of frosty air swept through the cabin as Honeysuckle replied, 'Aye aye, Captain,' and the hatch crashed shut.

Chapter Two

It was lovely when Rita was around for breakfast but Honeysuckle didn't mind being alone on The Patchwork Snail one tiny bit. She was used to it. Besides the little houseboat was so warm and welcoming; as Christmas was coming, Rita had hung more fairy lights through the saloon than there could possibly be in fairyland and the whole boat looked almost magical.

Honeysuckle hummed a selection of Abba tunes as she washed up the breakfast things. She hung the rose-printed mugs back on to their hooks above the minute sink and put the full, green enamel kettle on to the stove before squeezing herself into the bathroom.

As she washed herself and brushed her teeth, Honeysuckle admired the new 'artwork' that she and her mum had created on the wall above the basin. Another patch of mould had appeared a couple of weeks before and Rita and Honeysuckle had covered it up with a painting of a mermaid. The mermaid swam, smiling, amongst the many fishes and octopuses that covered up all the other damp patches on the walls. Her hair was dark and thick, like Honeysuckle's, as Rita thought dark paint would hide the mould better than yellow. Her tail was silvery green and curled around the edge of the basin, hiding a black mark that insisted on reappearing whatever Rita did to it.

Honeysuckle knew that her mum found it hard living on the canal but Honeysuckle loved it. She loved the sound of the water. Even when it was almost frozen, like this morning, it still sighed and shushed and gently rocked the boat. She loved the way the moonlight reflected back from the water's surface and sent ghostly ripples of light across the walls of her cabin. She loved it in the summer when they could leave the hatch open and the sunlight poured across her bunk and into the little saloon. And she loved it on dark, chilly mornings like this when the wood-burning stove crackled and chuckled and she could watch the icy day begin to dawn and sparkle in the wintry sun.

It was true that there wasn't much space on The

Patchwork Snail – most of their belongings had to be stored in a small blue shed near the boat. But then if there had been enough space to have her own dog, Honeysuckle might never have started the Dog Walkers' Club.

The kettle began to whistle and Honeysuckle poured boiling water over the fresh tea-leaves in the bottom of the rose-printed teapot. She left the tea to brew while she went back into her cabin and pulled on a pair of thick grass-green tights. Over these she fastened a short red wool skirt. Then she pulled on a multi-coloured striped jumper with yellow crocheted flowers patching holes on the elbows and finally put her green feet into her favourite pair of red, woolly-lined ankle boots. 'There!' she said, as she snapped a third sparkly clip into her tonne and a half of black curly hair. 'Just a bracelet or two . . . and then I'm ready!'

Every morning when Rita had left for work, Honeysuckle made herself a special cup of tea. This morning was no exception. When she had drunk the tea, Honeysuckle whirled the remains around in the bottom of the cup and then turned the cup upside down on to the saucer. This left just the tea-leaves in the bottom of the cup and from these tea-leaves Honeysuckle was convinced she could predict the future. OK, so she didn't *always* get it right – sometimes the shapes that the tea-leaves made were difficult to understand – but Honeysuckle was in no doubt that she had fortune-telling powers.

She peered into the depths of her teacup. Well, there was a dog there and that was certain! But the tea-leaves had made a sort of double dog, a bit like an inkblot picture; one dog was joined to the other by its paws! What on earth could that mean?

There wasn't much time to think about the tea-leaves, as Honeysuckle realised it was much later than she had thought. She had agreed to meet the other Dog Walkers outside Mrs Whitely-Grub's house across the road. She just had time to check in her registration book that she had the details of the morning's walk right (and to admire the number of entries that the book now held) before scrambling into her yellow duffle coat, pinning on her official homemade Dog Walkers' badge and bundling herself out of the hatch. This she secured after making sure that everything was shipshape and jumped off the edge of the houseboat on to dry land. As she jumped the boat shook and swayed and Honeysuckle thought briefly again about Sergeant Monmouth. Whenever he stamped on to the boat's deck it went on shivering about for ages as if it was recovering from a bad shock. She glanced at the canal and tried to forget the horrible stories he had told her the evening before. She knew it was mean of her to be upset about her mum going out with the Sergeant but Honeysuckle loved her life as it was – just her and her mum. She didn't want anything to change.

She scuttled across the garden towards the steps up to the street. Even the gnome that sat by their little shed had an icicle on the end of his nose – it really was very chilly.

'Hey, Abba freak!' called a voice. Honeysuckle looked across the road and saw her two very best girl friends and Billy waiting for her. They were standing at the end of Mrs Whitely-Grub's garden path stamping their feet and jumping up and down, trying to keep warm. Anita looked especially chilly. Honeysuckle suspected that she had already been to swimming training and probably hadn't had time to dry her hair properly. She had a woolly hat pulled down over her ears and the end of her nose was quite pink.

'Come on, slowcoach! We've been waiting ages,' said Jaime.

'Sorry,' said Honeysuckle. 'I forgot the time.'

'Bet you were doing the tea-leaf thing!' Jaime went on. 'Did you see anything interesting?'

The three friends gathered closely round Honeysuckle while she explained that she hadn't been quite certain what the sign in her teacup had meant but she knew it had something to do with dogs.

'Well, that's pretty obvious!' said Jaime. 'We've got four of them to walk this morning, haven't we?'

Jaime was dressed in her dungarees as usual. She had a khaki coat over the top and a big orange scarf wound round her neck. Honeysuckle could tell she had forgotten to brush her hair again. Jaime was such a tomboy – that was why she liked to hang out with Billy almost as much as she liked being with Honeysuckle and Anita. But as boys went Billy wasn't all that bad. He could be quite helpful with ideas for investigations into crimes; at least, he had been when the Dog Walkers had investigated a possible murder.

'Come on,' he said. 'Let's get Cupid and then pick up the others. We could take them down by the lake at the side of the canal – my mate told me that it's all frozen solid!'

'Great,' agreed the others as they set off up Mrs Whitely-Grub's garden path.

Chapter Three

It was hard to imagine now why Honeysuckle and her friends had ever thought that Mrs Whitely-Grub might be a murderer. She was such a sweet old lady really. She opened the red front door of her house and gave each of the Dog Walkers a beaming smile before handing them Cupid's pink python-skin lead. The little poodle came scuttling down the hall towards them.

'There you are, Cupie darling! Here are your lovely friends, come to take you for a walkies so that Mummy can go and get her shopping done. What a lucky little boysy woysy you are!'

To begin with Cupid hadn't been at all keen to go out with Honeysuckle and the others, but now that he knew them better he twizzled his little pompom tail like a propeller whenever the Dog Walkers arrived. They had got

15

used to him too by now. They knew that he would quite happily go down a rabbit hole if they let him and that it wasn't a good idea to take him on to The Patchwork Snail in case he got overexcited and peed on the furniture. This had already happened once and Honeysuckle didn't fancy a repeat performance. He had also taught them that it was a very good idea to have a supply of plastic bags in their pockets just in case one of the dogs did 'you know what' in the wrong place and the Dog Walkers had to do a poop scoop.

Today, however, it took a good deal of coaxing to persuade Cupid that a walk on that freezing morning was a good idea. As dogs went, Cupid was a bit of a wimp. What he liked best was to be snuggled up somewhere being fed yummy tit-bits, not having to go for a walk at all. He stood shivering on the doorstep and made pathetic whimpering noises.

'Oh dear,' said Honeysuckle, trying to lure him over the threshold with one of the small bone-shaped biscuits that she kept in her pocket.

'Don't worry, my dear!' exclaimed Mrs Whitely-Grub. 'I've got just the thing!' and she tottered off into her kitchen emerging a few moments later with a small package. 'I thought you might find it a teeny bit coldy woldy this morning so I bought you a little coat, didn't I, sweetie pie?' she said as she leaned down and fastened a small check coat around the little dog's tummy.

Honeysuckle wanted to laugh and she could hear Jaime snorting behind her, but instead she managed to say, 'Doesn't he look smart?' and bent over to pat Cupid's designer-coat-covered back before Mrs Whitely-Grub could see her grinning.

However funny he looked in it, the designer coat worked and Cupid was soon pottering, rather reluctantly, down the road. He was still shivering a bit and whimpered every now and again, but Honeysuckle was sure he was all right.

By the time they had collected the other three dogs, the Dog Walkers were all as warm as pie. They had needed to hurry after Cupid had held them up. Walking quickly through the small town brought roses to their cheeks and they were all enjoying puffing clouds of steamy breath out into the still air.

Although in her heart of hearts Honeysuckle had to admit that she liked Blossom the bloodhound the best, she let Billy walk her. Blossom was the biggest dog and Billy thought he would look a 'right wuss' if he was seen with a poodle or a Yorkshire terrier or even a sort of basset hound. So he went in front with Blossom while Honeysuckle and Jaime walked together with Cupid and Hamlet, and Anita came along behind with Pudding. Pudding had very short legs and a rather fat body so walking fast wasn't his best thing. Anita never minded being at the back; she had already swum dozens of lengths as part of her training for the county swimming team so she wasn't in need of exercise.

'So, tell me again what you saw in the tea-leaves this morning,' said Jaime, passing Hamlet's lead to her other hand so that Honeysuckle and she could walk side by side.

'It was very strange,' said Honeysuckle. 'It looked like a dog all right, but it was a sort of double dog – you know, like when you do an inkblot picture? It was a dog joined to another dog by its paws.'

'That sounds totally weird. And you have no idea what it could mean?' asked Jaime.

'Nope,' said Honeysuckle, as they rounded the corner that led them straight to the lake.

'This is amazing!' said Jaime when they reached the edge. 'I've never seen the water frozen solid like this. Shall we walk the dogs across it?' Jaime was a dare devil and loved taking risks, but Anita was the complete opposite.

'I don't think it's solid,' she said anxiously. 'Look, there's a sign over there that says, *Keep off the ice*. I don't think we should go on it at all.'

'Shame,' said Billy. 'I was going to come down later and test it to see how thick it is. My mate Alf's got some awesome skates . . .'

'Can I come?' asked Jaime.

'You mustn't skate on it, either of you!' said Anita. 'It could be dangerous!'

'It looks solid though,' said Jaime, peering into the lake. 'It would be amazing to have a slide . . .' She pressed the ice tentatively with the toe of her boot.

'Listen,' said Honeysuckle, pulling Jaime away from the edge, 'I think we better stick to the path while we've got the dogs – it would be dreadful if anything happened to any of them.'

'Exactly,' breathed Anita, looking relieved.

'Why don't we walk around the lake and let the dogs have a sniff at everything? There are sure to be some frozen puddles that we could slide on,' suggested Honeysuckle.

It was agreed that it would be too risky to go on to the ice while they had the dogs with them. In all honesty, they knew it would be stupid to go on it at all when there was a notice telling them quite clearly not to. So they kept all the dogs on their leads and set off round the perimeter of the lake.

Cupid was whimpering a lot by then, even though a pale lemon sun was glowing through the clouds. Honeysuckle decided to start singing so that she couldn't hear him. The others joined in and they sang 'Yellow Submarine' as they made their way along the path.

Honeysuckle was waving her hands about while singing the chorus just as Cupid decided that actually he had had enough of this walk. He turned and pulled suddenly at his lead. Honeysuckle spun round, hanging on tight. As she turned, she saw, standing in the middle of the ice, the thinnest, wispiest little dog imaginable.

'Look!' she shouted and the other Dog Walkers stopped to look in the direction that she was pointing.

'Where's he come from?' asked Anita.

'Over there!' said Honeysuckle as she and the other Dog Walkers spotted a small group of people standing at the edge of the lake about a hundred metres away.

'We've got to go and help,' said Jaime and they hurried towards them.

'I could easily slide out on to the ice and rescue him,' said Billy rather grandly while they jogged along.

'No, you couldn't,' gasped Anita. 'What if it broke and you fell in?'

'You would have to swim through the chunks of ice and rescue me and the dog,' said Billy. He was teasing Anita but she still looked miserable.

'I think he's frozen on to the ice,' said Honeysuckle as they got closer and then she gasped. She turned wide-eyed to look at the others. 'You know what this is, don't you?' Billy, Jaime and Anita looked puzzled. 'This is what I saw in the tea-leaves!' continued Honeysuckle. 'This is the inkblot dog that was there at the bottom of my teacup!'

'Wow!' breathed Billy. 'That is so cool!'

'It's more than cool,' said Jaime, giggling, 'it's *frozen*!'

'How can you laugh about that poor little dog?' asked Anita, her face all scrunched with worry. 'He might never be able to get back to the bank – he might die out there!'

She was looking so upset that Honeysuckle quickly said, 'Don't worry, we'll definitely think of some way to rescue him.'

They had nearly reached the group of people by now and one particular woman caught Honeysuckle's eye. The woman was thin and wispy, just like the dog on the ice. She was definitely the dog's owner because she was

21

looking so anxious. Her hands were clasped to her chest and her deep-set eyes were wide with fear. The woman was very, very pale and under her eyes there were bruise-coloured shadows. She was calling out in a trembling voice, 'Twitter, here boy, come,' but the little dog wasn't moving a single centimetre.

Honeysuckle knew that they had to do something fast. She felt dreadfully guilty – if only she had understood the sign in the tea-leaves properly, there might have been some way to stop Twitter from going on to the ice in the first place. She looked hard at the little dog. It was a whippet; she had seen a picture of a whippet in her dog training manual although she had never seen one in real life before. Even from this distance she could see that the little dog was shivering dreadfully.

'I just don't know what to do,' said the pale woman as the Dog Walkers reached the group of people. 'He won't move! I've called and called but he just won't budge . . .'

The woman looked as though she might be about to cry so Honeysuckle thought quickly. 'Please don't worry,' she said, 'I'm sure we will think of something.' Out of the corner of her eye she could see Billy coming out of the wooded area by the lake dragging a huge branch behind him.

'I'm going to push this out across the ice so that the dog can climb on to it and we can pull him back,' Billy said as he reached the others.

'What if he doesn't climb on to it?' asked Jaime.

'He will – I know he will,' said Billy confidently.

'I suppose it's worth a try,' said Honeysuckle doubtfully. As no one could think of any good reason why Billy shouldn't try to rescue Twitter with the branch, he began to push it out across the ice. Slowly, slowly he edged it nearer to Twitter. The whole group held its breath as they watched.

Twitter stared at the approaching branch, but as he leaned his nose towards it there was an ominous creaking sound.

'It's the ice,' squeaked Anita, 'the ice is going to break!' A moment later they could all hear the distinct sound of cracking.

'Quick,' shouted Honeysuckle, 'bring the branch back before it goes through!' She grabbed hold of Billy and reached across to help him pull it back to the bank.

'Phew,' gasped Anita when the branch was safely off the ice. 'That was so scary. Do you think the ice will hold? What if that poor little dog falls through now?'

'Shh!' hissed Honeysuckle not wanting to make

Twitter's owner any more frightened. 'Of course it will hold,' she said firmly even though she could so easily imagine the whippet disappearing into the blackness of the frozen lake. 'Thank goodness you didn't go on to the ice, Billy,' she whispered. Honeysuckle reached into her duffle coat pocket and pulled out one of the bone-shaped biscuits. 'I've got another idea.' She skidded the biscuit across the ice towards Twitter. The biscuit stopped several centimetres from where the dog stood. He whimpered pathetically before pushing his nose forward towards the biscuit. Honeysuckle bit her lip. Would Twitter be able to move? Would he take a step towards the biscuit and his owner without going through the ice?

After what felt like a lifetime Twitter took a trembling step. The whole group let out a sigh. Twitter wasn't frozen to the ice as they had all feared. The ice was silent as he sniffed at the biscuit and moved a little closer. His owner called encouragingly to him, 'Come on, boy, good boy,' but the dog had stopped again.

'How are we going to get him to come all the way across?' asked Jaime.

'You could keep throwing biscuits for him,' said Anita, 'but make sure that they land closer to us each time.'

'Or I could attach a piece of string to a biscuit and throw it out to him,' Honeysuckle replied. 'Then when he is just about to eat it, I could pull it closer and closer and . . .'

'Or I could lasso him!' said Billy. The others turned to look at him.

'*Could* you lasso him?' asked Honeysuckle, secretly feeling annoyed that she hadn't thought of that. 'What would you lasso him with?'

'Oh,' said Billy, looking crestfallen. 'I dunno.'

There was a moment's silence before Honeysuckle said excitedly, 'Oh, but I do! We could tie all the leads together and make a lasso out of them!'

'Ace plan!' said Billy, who was already unfastening Blossom's lead. Jaime, Anita and Honeysuckle did the same and asked the people standing nearby to hold on to the dogs while they clipped the leads together. Billy then managed to make a loop at one end using a piece of string that he had in his pocket.

As it had been his idea, it only seemed fair to let Billy try and catch Twitter first. Anyway, boys always think they are best at that sort of thing. The girls watched as he tried once, twice, three times to catch the dog.

Finally Honeysuckle said, 'Can I have a go?' and Billy

reluctantly gave her the makeshift lasso.

She swung the lasso round her head just as she had seen cowboys do in Westerns on TV and then she threw it. By a stroke of extraordinary luck, Twitter chose that moment to turn his head to the left and the loop of the lasso landed neatly round his neck! There was a muttered 'Amazing!' from the small crowd, although Billy said absolutely nothing.

Honeysuckle pulled gently on the leads and the dog began to move shakily across the ice. Everyone was terrified in case the ice broke and nobody made a sound.

It was all right! Twitter was so light that his weight made no difference – the ice was holding.

A cheer went up from the onlookers as the brilliant Dog Walkers pulled Twitter on to the bank. Honeysuckle felt herself blush with pride at the successful rescue and she smiled broadly to her audience.

'That was a really good idea,' she said kindly to Billy and he grinned.

'Thanks,' he said as they returned the shivering little dog to its owner.

Chapter Four

'What did you say this woman's name was?' asked Rita on the evening of The Rescue. She and Honeysuckle were snuggled in the saloon of The Patchwork Snail drinking hot tea and eating warm, buttery crumpets. Rita had taken off her biker boots and was warming her toes by the wood-burning stove. Although it was beautifully cosy she had tied a red shawl over her clothes and secured it on one shoulder. Her head was wrapped up in an electric blue scarf. Honeysuckle thought her mum looked like an exotic Eastern princess.

'Ms Moribunda,' said Honeysuckle, 'and the whippet is called Twitter. We have agreed to take him out for a walk tomorrow.'

'Well done, Honeybunch!' said Rita, making her

chandelier earrings swing enthusiastically. 'Another new client – how exciting!'

'Yes,' said Honeysuckle doubtfully. 'The thing is . . .'

'What?' asked Rita. 'What is "the thing"?'

'The thing is,' Honeysuckle went on, 'that there is something – er – something a bit, well, sort of *creepy* about her . . .'

'Creepy?' Rita snorted with laughter. Before she had stopped giggling, The Patchwork Snail began to rock and shudder and moments later they heard a loud knock on the hatch.

'I wonder who that can be!' said Rita, jumping up to open it.

Honeysuckle muttered under her breath, 'I bet I know . . .' and sure enough she was right. Sergeant Monmouth came plodding into the saloon and squeezed himself on to the bench seat next to Honeysuckle.

'Evenin' all!' he said and roared with laughter. He always said 'Evenin' all' when he arrived and for some reason he found this funny. Rita laughed too but Honeysuckle didn't. She couldn't for the life of her imagine what her mum saw in him.

'Well, well,' he said as he unbuttoned his overcoat

and made himself comfortable. 'What's going on here then, ladies?'

'We were just having a private chat,' said Honeysuckle rather rudely.

Rita scowled at her and began to tell Sergeant Monmouth all about the Dog Walkers' brave and brilliant rescue of Twitter the whippet. The Sergeant had to agree that it was an excellent achievement.

'And then,' Rita continued, 'Honeysuckle was approached by the owner of the whippet who she thought looked "creepy"!'

Honeysuckle was furious. How *dare* her mum tell Sergeant Monmouth secret things that she didn't want anyone else to know?

'What's her name and where does she live, then, this lady and her whippet?' the Sergeant asked, peering round at Honeysuckle. She could feel her cheeks burning. Why was he questioning her as if she was a criminal? It wasn't any of his business!

She looked down at the floor and mumbled, 'Her name is Ms Moribunda and she lives at Number 13 The Oaks . . .'

'And she looks "creepy" does she?' bellowed Sergeant Monmouth with a great big grin on his face. 'Ah . . .'

He went on sucking air through his teeth. 'In the past there were a lot of strange goings on in that part of town . . .'

'What?' gasped Honeysuckle. 'What sort of "goings on"?' As soon as she had asked she wished that she hadn't. She and the Dog Walkers had to go to that part of town the following day and she wasn't sure that she wanted to hear anything horrible . . . But Sergeant Monmouth was off on one of his long stories about the terrible things that had happened there.

'The thing is,' he began, 'that neck of the woods has a history . . .'

Before Honeysuckle could interrupt and say that she didn't want to know what it was, he went on.

'Oh yes . . . a strange and tragic history. A wealthy merchant back in the eighteenth century built a large house there. He had made his fortune importing silk from the east – had an eye for beautiful things, so the story goes . . . beautiful things and beautiful women.' Sergeant Monmouth paused for dramatic effect. Honeysuckle couldn't see that there was anything very strange or tragic about his story so far but then he continued. 'Yes, the wealthy merchant liked to be surrounded by beauty but he didn't like to share what he owned. He kept his treasures locked away for fear of being burgled and he never invited anyone into his home.

'One day he met a ravishing young woman who was sweetness itself. The merchant made up his mind on the spot that he would have to own this lovely creature. He talked to her father and it was agreed that the merchant would marry the young girl. Harriet, her name was, Harriet Fielding . . .' Sergeant Monmouth cleared his throat and continued. 'She was so beautiful that as soon as she had moved into the merchant's house he began to feel jealous. He didn't want anyone to see his lovely bride, he wanted to keep her all to himself, so . . .'

Honeysuckle couldn't help herself. 'So what?' she asked with her eyes wide. 'So what did he do?'

'First,' said Sergeant Monmouth, 'he locked all the doors so that she couldn't go out and no one could come in. Harriet began to grow thin and unhappy but the merchant was becoming more and more jealous, so next he blacked out all the windows. No one could look in and see his beautiful wife but she couldn't see out. She became paler and paler . . . Finally the merchant couldn't bear the thought that even his servants might look at Harriet, so do you know what he did . . .?' The

Sergeant looked from Rita to Honeysuckle. Both were sitting as still as statues with their eyes riveted to Sergeant Monmouth. There wasn't a sound except the crackle of the wood burner and the creak of the boat.

'What did he do?' breathed Rita.

'The story goes that the merchant drugged Harriet and left her deeply asleep upstairs while he set about opening up a cavity behind the fireplace in his living room. He took away brick after brick until there was enough space to hide a person. Then he went back up to his wife's bedroom and carried her sleeping body down . . .' Sergeant Monmouth paused. 'He put his beautiful, young, slumbering wife in the space behind the fireplace and slowly and deliberately replaced all of the bricks.'

'What happened to her?' gasped Honeysuckle, feeling the hairs stand up on the back of her neck.

'No one ever found her,' Sergeant Monmouth sighed. 'It's said that on certain nights the ghost of the poor young girl can still be heard to this day crying and scratching behind the fireplace, begging to be let out . . . The merchant went mad eventually. Got rid of all his servants and spent his time wandering from room to room. Perhaps he was searching for his bride, who knows? The rotted remains of his body were found many years later.'

'Well!' said Rita, suddenly wanting to change the subject as she saw Honeysuckle shudder. 'Of course that's a lot of nonsense, isn't it, Sergeant? Now, what about a nice hot cup of tea? Do you fancy a crumpet?'

'Don't mind if I do,' the Sergeant replied. 'I don't know about it being "nonsense" as you say; a lot of strange things happen in this town, I can tell you!'

Please *don't* tell me, thought Honeysuckle but it was too late.

'So what's been going on today then?' Rita asked brightly.

'Another break-in at the Pig and Whistle – took the one-armed bandit this time and smashed the place up a bit just for good measure!'

'How awful!' said Rita.

'And that Mrs Pomfrey from the posh estate has lost her precious pedigree Persian cat – says it's been stolen – worth a blooming fortune apparently.'

'You don't say!' said Rita.

'And Sergeant Bottomly's had his bike half-inched again!' Rita looked puzzled. 'Half-inched – pinched!' explained Sergeant Monmouth, grinning, and then he launched into another horrible story about a man on a bike in the High Street who got flattened like a kipper by a steam roller several years ago. But Honeysuckle wasn't listening any more – she was thinking about the following day and Harriet Fielding.

Chapter Five

Honeysuckle snapped to her senses when Sergeant Monmouth got up to leave. She couldn't bear to think about Harriet Fielding being bricked into a chimney and she knew she had to put the whole, stupid story out of her head.

She must have looked worried though, because as he climbed back up the steps to the hatch Sergeant Monmouth called out, 'And remember, ladies, you've nothing to fear when Monmouth is near!'

Rita giggled and Honeysuckle heard the two of them make a date to go out. She shivered and thought to herself, How can he say nothing to fear when he is near? I didn't have anything to fear *until* he showed up, now he's made me feel like jelly!

'Oooh, I don't know, those stories!' Rita exclaimed,

plonking herself back down next to Honeysuckle when the Sergeant had finally gone. 'I don't know where he gets them from or why he thinks we want to hear them!'

'He probably thinks he's really interesting,' said Honeysuckle grumpily and then she muttered under her breath, 'He goes on so much he ought to be called Sergeant Motormouth.' Rita didn't hear, she had jumped up again and was clattering the mugs away and filling the little sink with soapy water.

'He didn't upset you, did he?' she asked in a rather shrill voice.

'Nope,' said Honeysuckle.

'It's all a lot of rubbish, you know,' Rita said, 'but I have to tell you that he has left me gasping for a ciggie . . . do you think one little puff would matter? Just to steady my nerves?'

'Yes, it would matter,' said Honeysuckle. 'Chew some of that special gum. Anyway why do you need to steady your nerves if Sergeant Monmouth's stories are all a lot of rubbish?'

'Oh, it's not the *stories*,' gasped Rita. 'No, no, it's nothing to do with the stories – it's him. It makes me jittery having a policeman here – there isn't room really, is there? Now, if we lived in a nice little house on the estate, that would be different.'

Honeysuckle looked horrified but Rita didn't notice. Honeysuckle really hoped that her mum wasn't upset about where they lived. No, Rita was probably upset for just the same reason as Honeysuckle herself – the stupid story about the merchant's house had given them both the shivers.

It was getting late. Honeysuckle stood up and stretched. 'I'm going to get ready for bed now,' she said, stifling a pretend yawn. 'I'm really sleepy and I think I'll have a bath.' She was hoping that a warm, comforting soak in the little 'ice cream tub' would calm her down and help her sleep better. Even though Rita often got fed up with their tiny bathroom, Honeysuckle thought it was the best one in the world; small, yes, but friendly and way more exciting than any other bathroom she had been in.

But on this particular night when she got into the bath and looked around the walls of the bathroom, she was convinced that she saw the mermaid smile in a nasty, sneering way and flick her tail. Honeysuckle peered closer through the steam but the mermaid had stopped moving. She shut her eyes and lay back as best she could in the hot, bubbly water. Ahhh, she thought, that's better . . . except . . . She opened her eyes wide. Except that I can smell cigarette smoke! Mum's smoking and it's that stupid Motormouth's fault for scaring us like that! Why did he have to come round and spoil everything? Mum hasn't had a ciggie in ages and now look what's happened!

Honeysuckle dried herself and put on her red starry pyjamas; she decided not to mention the cigarette to her mum. She was certain that it was only a little slip and that the next day everything would be fine again. Instead she called out 'Night!' as cheerily as she could and closed her cabin door.

She went to pull the spotty curtains across her window. On any other night she would just have pulled them and that would have been that, but this evening was different. She felt she had to check that there was nothing weird going on outside.

Honeysuckle put her nose to the window and gazed out into the darkness. There was a full moon and the sky was crystal clear. The canal was almost frozen and the moonlight glittered across the surface. It was so beautiful that for a moment Honeysuckle felt comforted, but, suddenly, a movement on the other side of the canal caught her eye. Was there a figure hiding in the trees? A figure all in black – a figure that appeared to be almost floating rather than walking! 'Eeeek!' she squealed softly to herself. 'What *is* that?' She saw a ghostly light coming from the figure, a pale, shimmering, flickering light. It paused and flashed and in an instant Honeysuckle could see that there was another figure behind the first except that this one was crawling on all fours!

She rubbed her eyes and looked again. 'Oh for goodness' sake!' she said out loud. 'It's just someone walking their dog and carrying a torch so that they can see where they're going!' She giggled and pulled the curtains tight shut. 'Honeysuckle Lovelace,' she said fiercely to herself, 'you have got to stop all this nonsense and get straight into your bunk and go to sleep!'

She obeyed the first part of her instructions easily, but the going to sleep part was much more difficult. She left her fairy lights on – the twinkling coloured flowers were comforting – but had The Patchwork Snail always made such strange noises? So many creakings and groanings? Honeysuckle was certain that it hadn't. She decided that the best thing to do was to put her head under the covers and recite the words of as many Abba songs to herself as she could possibly remember and not to think for one second about Motormouth, his stupid stories or her mum's date with him. And she absolutely wouldn't think about Rita saying that she wanted to live in a house on dry land.

Eventually she did fall into a strange, fitful sleep. Poor Honeysuckle; even her dreams were full of horrors. Abba turned into monsters and threatened to eat her and the other Dog Walkers if they couldn't sing all their songs backwards. While they were trying to do that, the ice they were standing on cracked and the water around them was full of shivering whippets and the monsters were getting closer and closer . . .

'Wakey, wakey, sleepyhead,' a voice called in Honeysuckle's dream, and then she felt a kiss on her forehead and opened her eyes to see Rita beaming down at her. 'Come on you!' she said. 'I've got to go to work now and you're not even awake!'

'Oh,' said Honeysuckle, dragging herself out of her bunk. 'What time is it?'

'Late!' said Rita. 'I've got to go . . . you'll be OK today, Honeybunch?'

'Yeah,' said Honeysuckle, 'and you will too, won't you? Don't go and smoke or anything!' She caught the guilty look in Rita's eyes.

'Absolutely not,' Rita replied, and whooshed herself and her huge pink plastic earrings out through the hatch. 'Leave everything shipshape!' she called from the top.

'Aye aye, Captain,' Honeysuckle called back before she stumbled into the galley kitchen to make herself a cup of tea.

She sat on the faded green velvet bench and hugged herself while she waited for the kettle to boil. Her head was full of cobwebs and spooks. She was jumpy and tired at the same time and nothing felt right. The Patchwork Snail looked the same but it was different somehow, not quite so familiar, not quite so friendly.

Honeysuckle shook herself and set about making tea. As she sipped the fragrant brew she began to feel a little better. By the time the cup was finished she felt strong enough to read the tea-leaves. She swirled and tipped the cup as usual, but the shape that was left by the tea-leaves did nothing to comfort her. It was a strange, bundled shape; a shape Honeysuckle couldn't make sense of. It was a ghostly shape.

When the others arrived at The Patchwork Snail ready to go to Number 13 The Oaks, Honeysuckle had dressed herself in all her brightest clothes. She had put tinsel and ribbons through her hair and pushed thirteen different coloured glass bangles on to her arms. The bangles made a cheerful chinking sound when she moved and the tinsel glittered wonderfully, but Honeysuckle still didn't feel right. She had, however, made up her mind not to tell Jaime or Billy and especially not Anita anything about Motormouth's stupid story. And the idea that her mum might want to move from The Patchwork Snail was too horrible to say out loud.

They all noticed straight away that Honeysuckle wasn't her usual bouncy self. She was so quiet and so pale. Anita put her arm round Honeysuckle's shoulders and whispered, 'Is everything all right?'

Honeysuckle answered her bravely. 'Yes, yes! Absolutely, positively and completely all right!'

Chapter Six

Anita kept her arm around Honeysuckle's shoulders while they all made their way to Number 13 The Oaks. They need not all have come really – after all there was only one little dog to take out – but it was as if none of them had felt it would be fair to make one person go on their own. Besides, no one had anything better to do and it was always fun getting to know a new client.

The sky had lightened and a brilliant sun was glittering off the frost-laden trees and rooftops. There was a feeling of excitement in the air, a feeling of magic and expectation; the sort of feeling that really only comes just before Christmas.

Honeysuckle and Anita walked in step, then they began to do little jumps and hops and dance moves as they went along. Honeysuckle grinned; it was such a beautiful day, how could she possibly have imagined that anything creepy was going to happen? There was nothing in the least bit spooky about a sparkling day like today. She tried to forget all about her mum and Sergeant Monmouth. And she did her best to forget the ghostly shape she had seen in the tea-leaves – she had probably got it wrong; she did *sometimes* misread the signs, after all. She thought how bonkers she had been even to think for a moment that Motormouth hadn't made up the whole silly story about the mad, bad merchant and his poor wife.

The four Dog Walkers turned left off the bright, sunny main street into The Oaks. They had been humming in harmony but now they stopped instantly. Honeysuckle and Anita stood still. The sun had suddenly disappeared, the whole street was in shadow and it was so cold.

'Brrrr!' said Jaime. 'It's dead gloomy down here, isn't it?'

'It's because the houses are really tall and these huge trees don't help either,' said Billy.

They looked up at the houses around them. They were indeed very tall, with sharp sloping roofs and dark-coloured doors and window frames. The windows themselves were arched and pointed almost like church windows. Although each house was different in style from the others, they were all made of the same dark grey brick.

'Ugh! It's horrid down here – really creepy. Which is Number 13 do you think?' asked Anita.

'It's that one, over there,' said Jaime, who was fearlessly marching ahead of the others.

'Whoa!' said Anita, dropping back behind Honeysuckle. 'That's the creepiest of the lot!'

'Don't be daft,' said Jaime. 'It's just a *house*.'

'I expect it's full of ghouls and ghosts and two-headed monsters,' said Billy, making his freakiest face and jabbing at Anita with his fingers. Poor Anita was so easy to tease and Billy loved making fun of her. 'They'll all come out and eat you!' he cackled as he grabbed her from behind and made her shriek.

'Stop it!' said Honeysuckle, feeling horribly wobbly. 'We've got to at least try and look professional – after all, Twitter is a new client . . .'

'You're right,' said Billy. 'Sorry, I was just larking around. Come on, Anita, why don't you go and knock on the gateway to hell!'

'Shut up, Billy,' Jaime snapped. She wasn't feeling

quite so confident any more. 'If you're so brave, you go first – go on!'

'OK,' said Billy. 'I will!' He didn't go straight away though. Billy, like the others, stood at the end of the tiled path that led up to the dark oak front door and surveyed the house for a minute or two. They stared at the pointed roof and the many blank-looking windows that showed no curtains or light of any kind. They looked at the chocolate brown paint, which was peeling from the window frames, and the cobwebby spear-headed railings surrounding the house. There was nothing much in the front garden – at least, nothing much that was alive. The only living thing was a huge yew hedge that virtually covered the downstairs windows. It looked black and menacing.

'Go on, then,' said Jaime again, looking at Billy.

And this time he did set off up the garden path. The girls followed a little way behind.

'I think I need to go home, I'm sure there's something I've forgotten to do . . .' Anita whispered to Honeysuckle, as they got closer to the front door.

'No, there isn't,' Honeysuckle hissed back, holding on tightly to Anita's hand. 'It's all going to be fine, you'll see . . .'

Billy pushed the blackened brass bell and they heard the ring echo through the house. Anita tried to pull away from Honeysuckle but she held on tight.

Moments later, the huge door creaked open and there in the doorway stood Ms Moribunda herself. She looked so tiny in the vast doorway and her eyes seemed even more deeply sunken than Honeysuckle remembered; her skin was thin like tissue paper stretched over her skull. She smiled a wan little smile and wished them all 'Good morning'. Honeysuckle, Jaime, Anita and Billy did their best to say, 'Good morning' back without sounding too shaky.

'It's so good of you to come,' Ms Moribunda continued. 'I know that Twitter will be delighted to be taken out. I haven't got time to walk him properly today, what with visiting estate agents and solicitors. I'll just call him, wait a moment.' She turned and walked back into the cavernous hallway.

'She looks almost *haunted*, doesn't she?' whispered Jaime while she was gone.

Honeysuckle bit her tongue; she was not going to tell them Sergeant Motormouth's stupid story about this part of town, even though she was beginning to feel that there might have been a grain of truth in it.

Just then, Ms Moribunda returned with Twitter by her side. The little whippet was so skinny and small and his eyes were bulging as if he was terrified. Ms Moribunda handed his lead to Billy. 'There you are,' she said. 'Shall we say a couple of hours?'

'OK,' said Billy, doing his best to smile cheerfully.

'We'll look after him very carefully,' said Honeysuckle, trying to control the butterflies in her stomach.

'I'm sure you will,' said Ms Moribunda. 'Thank you so much.' And with that the huge door creaked and crashed shut again.

'Quick!' said Anita. 'Let's get out of here!' She scuttled back down the gloomy path and into the street. The others followed and for a short while Twitter fidgeted along beside them.

With great relief they reached the sun-filled common and once again Honeysuckle pushed the thought of Motormouth and his story to the back of her mind.

Twitter wasn't at all easy to walk. He twitched and trembled so much that it was almost impossible to make any progress. Honeysuckle tried throwing a stick for him but he just quivered and gazed at her with his prominent eyes. When they let him off the lead he didn't take a single step. They had only been out for about ten minutes and already Twitter seemed to have had enough. Although the sun was shining it was still cold and the poor little dog shivered and shook so much that eventually Billy picked him up and wrapped him in his scarf.

'Oh that's better!' said Anita. 'Look at him! He's much happier now.'

Honeysuckle could only gasp and grin. The little dog certainly did look much happier. He also looked remarkably like the bundle shape that she had seen in her tea-leaves! The tea-leaves weren't trying to tell her that something spooky was going to happen – they were telling her that instead of walking, Twitter would prefer being wrapped up and carried!

'What are you grinning at?' asked Jaime.

'Oh nothing! Just that I got my tea-leaves a bit wrong this morning, that's all! Shall we take it in turns to carry Twitter until it's time to go back?' she said, changing the subject.

And that is exactly what they did. Everything was absolutely fine until they got back to Number 13 The Oaks. When Billy handed Twitter back to Ms Moribunda he explained that the little dog had preferred to be carried than walk in the cold air. It was then that Ms Moribunda said, 'I did wonder if that might be the case. He can be funny with people he doesn't know very well.' She tickled the dog's ear fondly. 'I have so many errands to do tomorrow and I don't like to leave him here on his own. I can't take him all round town with me – I don't suppose one or even all of you would be able to come here and sit with Twitter tomorrow afternoon, would you? I have to be out for several hours and it would be such a comfort to know that he had company.'

Before Honeysuckle could speak, Billy said that he and Jaime were playing football the following afternoon and Anita hurriedly said that she had a training session at the local swimming pool. Ms Moribunda looked appealingly at Honeysuckle and the others turned to stare at her too. Honeysuckle swallowed hard and found herself saying shakily, 'I could come.'

Chapter Seven

'Can't wait to hear what the inside of that place is like,' said Billy on their way to Jaime's house. 'The outside looks like something out of a horror movie, all dark and menacing! And did you hear how Ms Moribunda's footsteps echoed down the hall?'

'Oh Billy, stop it. Poor Honeysuckle!' Anita groaned.

'You're not going to wimp out, are you, Honeysuckle?' Billy asked her. 'Not like our swimmer here!' He pointed unkindly at Anita.

'No,' said Honeysuckle firmly. 'Anyway what do you mean about Anita?' She turned to look at her friend.

Anita mumbled. 'Um . . . I *might* have swimming practice tomorrow afternoon.'

'You're such a fibber,' said Jaime, smiling at her. 'You

told me that you weren't doing any more training until after Christmas.'

'I'd forgotten I'd told you that!' The others, including Billy, laughed. 'I'm sorry,' Anita said, turning to Honeysuckle. 'I don't have swimming practice tomorrow and . . . and I *could* come with you, if you really wanted me to.'

'It's all right,' said Honeysuckle bravely. 'I'll be OK on my own.' In all honesty she thought that it would be easier to be alone at Number 13 The Oaks than to have to try and keep Anita calm as well. It would have been great if they had all been going, though. Well, maybe not great but better at least.

'It's just that Number 13 looks so creepy,' said Anita anxiously, squeezing Honeysuckle's arm.

'And you're a wimp,' said Billy, grinning this time and giving Anita a tickle. He hadn't meant to be unkind to her, but he couldn't bear it when people didn't tell the truth. He was kicking a stone along the street. 'Everyone knows that there are no such things as ghosts!'

'He's right!' said Honeysuckle firmly, so firmly in fact that Jaime turned to stare at her. 'Stories about ghosts are just a lot of silly rubbish,' she said, not meeting Jaime's eye. 'Everyone knows they're all made up by stupid people with nothing between their ears!' She almost growled the last bit and even Billy looked surprised. 'Anyway,' she said, realising that she might have gone too far, 'Ms Moribunda has paid us for today so why don't we use the money to get something to eat and take it back to Jaime's?'

'OK,' the others agreed happily.

When they were all safely settled into the ramshackle kitchen in Jaime's home, the Dog Walkers settled down to eat their crusty rolls and hot tomato soup. Honeysuckle had brought the registration book with her. It was open on the floor and they were adding up the number of clients that they had. Word had spread quickly and their homemade posters in Curl Up and Dye and the local newsagents had brought in plenty of new dog owners. There were nine dogs that they walked quite regularly now and adding Twitter made a grand total of ten.

'There should be plenty of work before Christmas,' said Honeysuckle, 'when people want to go out for the day to do their shopping.' She thought about how much money she would be able to give her mum to help keep The Patchwork Snail repaired and hoped that she wouldn't mention moving again.

As she thought about The Patchwork Snail, Honeysuckle looked round Jaime's kitchen. You could probably have fitted the whole of the Lovelaces' house-boat into this one room. There were cupboards and shelves everywhere and each one was bulging or sagging with belongings. Honeysuckle thought about how much she liked The Patchwork Snail when it was all shipshape with everything put neatly in its own place. She didn't miss having lots of space to put things and she wasn't even envious of Jaime's bedroom, which had two beds in it and a wardrobe and huge bookcase. She loved her tiny cabin and she *could* have a friend to stay as long as they didn't mind sleeping on the floor in a sleeping bag by her bunk.

'How much are you going to charge to sit with Twitter?' asked Anita, snapping Honeysuckle out of her daydream. Anita herself had been dreaming that she would earn enough money one day to build her own swimming pool.

'Loads,' said Billy. 'She'll need danger money in case she gets *scared to death*!' he hissed into Anita's ear.

'You're such a twit, Billy,' said Honeysuckle fiercely, 'but I think we could charge a little bit more for house-sitting as well as dog-sitting, don't you?'

'Too right!' said Billy. He stood up and brushed the crumbs off his jeans. 'Listen, I've gotta go – I promised my mum I'd help her with the shopping and she'll be expecting me. Good luck tomorrow at The House of the Living Dead!' He hooted with laughter as he bounded across the kitchen to the back door.

'See you!' the others shouted and he banged the door shut.

Honeysuckle never minded having Billy around – he could be really funny when he wasn't being a twit – but somehow when it was just her and Anita and Jaime it was even nicer. They could talk about girly things without annoying Billy. Even though Jaime was a bit of a tomboy, she still loved dressing up and making tiaras out of tinsel and beads. Sometimes when it was only the three of them they would make up new dance routines. This was quite difficult in the saloon of the boat where there was so little room that they often ended up falling over each other and getting dreadful giggles. But here, in Jaime's huge kitchen, they could leap and jiggle as much as they wanted.

When they had danced themselves to a standstill Honeysuckle wanted to do something else to take her mind off Number 13 The Oaks and the scary thought of being inside the house the following day. 'I know,' she said. 'Has your mum got any old magazines we could cut up?'

'Yeah,' said Jaime, jumping up. 'She's got stacks of them ready to be recycled.' Jaime's mum worked for a fashion stylist, although you would never guess it to look at Jaime. She seemed to have decided to be the opposite of her mum and go around in a permanent state of grunge. Jaime staggered back into the kitchen from the hallway with a pile of glossy magazines under her arm.

'What do you want to do with them?' she asked.

'Let's cut out all the jewellery,' said Honeysuckle, 'and stick it on ourselves so that it looks like we're wearing real diamonds and things!'

'Brilliant!' the others agreed and they set to work. As they snipped and chatted Honeysuckle forgot all about ghosts and her mum and the Sergeant and the horrible idea of moving.

The sun was already going down and the kitchen began to glow in the fading light. The girls decked themselves out with paper necklaces, earrings and huge rock-like rings. They made up stories about the fabulous parties they were about to go to wearing all their sumptuous jewels. They described to each other what their dresses would be like and how many thousands of pounds each shimmering gown would cost.

By the time Honeysuckle got back to The Patchwork Snail she had passed at least three hours without thinking once about Number 13 The Oaks.

'Oooh!' Rita squealed when she crashed her way back through the hatch. She gawped at Honeysuckle, who was still all decked in her paper jewels. 'Don't you look gorgeous? My favourite thing – masses of bling!' and then she collapsed dramatically on to the bench. She stretched herself out as far as she could without actually bashing into anything and kicked off her charity shop gold ballroom-dancing shoes. She had on silver lurex tights and her big toe was poking through on one foot. Her toenail was painted metallic purple, which was pretty much the colour of her short, full skirt. From under her skirt, layers and layers of pink net just showed. On top, Rita wore a silvery grey jumper that she had found in Oxfam the week before; it had huge beaded stars all round the neck and when she raised her arms above her head, a small expanse of leopard-print vest peeped out from underneath. Her earrings were cascades of silver beads and hung almost down to her shoulders. Honeysuckle thought she looked like a fairy. She was proud of her mum. She loved the way she dressed and she loved finding bargains in the charity shops with her. She knew her friends thought she was amazing too.

'You would not believe how many grey roots I've touched up today!' Rita wheezed. 'Honestly, it seems like everyone and her dog wants to look younger for the holidays – sometimes I look at all the old biddies and think, Why bother? Why not let Mother Nature take her course and just say "to hell with it, let the world see me grey and grizzled!" But then I suppose there wouldn't be so much for yours truly to do, would there?' She gave a huge shrug before going on. 'Oh – talking of everyone and her dog – how was your new client?'

It was as if Honeysuckle had been kicked in the stomach. She had been so happy, so warm and comfortable and having so much fun and now . . . there was the thought of that horrible house again.

'Oh,' she said, 'you know . . . all right, really. Twitter is a lovely dog,' she went on. 'I'm going to dog-sit in Ms Moribunda's house tomorrow – which is going to be *fine*,' she finished emphatically.

'Good,' said Rita, looking hard at Honeysuckle. Honeysuckle looked the other way. Rita then changed the subject and made them both a cup of hot chocolate.

Neither Honeysuckle nor her mum mentioned Number 13 The Oaks, the Sergeant or moving to a house again that evening. Instead they listened to stories on the radio and made paper chains to hang across the ceiling of The Patchwork Snail. They ate spaghetti with sauce for supper and roasted chestnuts in the wood burner until it was time for bed.

As she closed the door of her cabin, Honeysuckle wondered whether she should consult her crystal ball, just in case it could give her some clue about the following day and what to expect. If she was honest, she hadn't seen much in its shiny depths so far but she was certain that with practice she would be able to see more and more. She pulled out the drawer under her bunk and rummaged around until she felt the soft, beaded velvet covering that kept the crystal ball safe. She lifted it out and stood the ball on its wooden stand. Then she carefully opened up the velvet.

She had to be certain that Rita wouldn't come in. Her mum would be furious if she knew what Honeysuckle was doing; she called anything to do with fortune-telling a lot of old mumbo jumbo, especially as it reminded her of Honeysuckle's dad. So that her mum would think she was asleep, Honeysuckle turned off the light by her bed; she didn't even leave the fairy lights on. She would be able to see by the light of the full moon that slithered in through her window. She took a deep breath and peered into the centre of the ball . . .

'Uh?' she gasped and pushed her nose closer to the shiny surface. 'What *is* that?' she whispered. 'It's grey . . . and fuzzy . . . and shapeless . . .' Then the image was gone. Honeysuckle leaned back in her chair and whispered into the shivering stillness of the moonlit air. 'It was completely, absolutely, positively – a GHOST!'

Chapter Eight

'I think I'll rearrange my bookshelf,' Honeysuckle muttered to herself the following day, glancing round her tiny cabin. 'I've already organised all my hair bobbles and my bangles, I've tidied my clothes – sort of – and put clean sheets on my bed . . . what else can I do?' She hummed a bit while she set to work on the tiny blue bookshelf above her minute dressing table.

She had to fill the time somehow. Rita had gone to work hours ago and there was still at least another hour before she needed to leave. Honeysuckle would have liked to lie down on her bunk and have a snooze, but she was much too jumpy for snoozing. She had hardly slept a wink the night before. All she could think about was the ghostly shape that had appeared in her crystal ball and what it might mean. Except that she knew what it meant – she knew it was an omen, warning her that Number 13 The Oaks was . . . 'NO!' Honeysuckle shouted at herself. 'You are NOT going to be scared by that stupid, potty, dotty, crazy story that stupid, potty, dotty, crazy Motormouth told you . . . stop it AT ONCE!' She was rather pleased with how fierce she sounded so she carried on a bit more. 'You know full well that his ridiculous story was all nonsense and, even if it wasn't, it probably had nothing whatsoever to do with Number 13 The Oaks . . . I command you not to think about it any more!'

Hmm! she thought to herself, So there! I wish I had talked like that to Motormouth! And while she carefully dusted and straightened the small collection of books that fitted on her shelf she began to think more about Sergeant Motormouth himself. Could her mum really like him that much? Was he the reason that Rita had mentioned moving to a house? Because there wouldn't be room for a big, fat policeman on The Patchwork Snail and she wanted him to move in? Oh please, thought Honeysuckle, she *couldn't* want that! She would have to listen to his gruesome stories *every day* and she and her mum would never be on their own together any more. Honeysuckle would have to leave this houseboat that she loved so much and live in a boring old brick house just like everyone else. She felt miserable at the thought of it.

She pulled out one of her favourite books. She would cuddle herself into her duvet and settle down in the saloon to read until it was time to go. She plumped up the brightly coloured cushions that were scattered across the bench seat and folded herself into the corner. Although it was quite a bright day, all the fairy lights were on and the paper chains looked cheerful and festive. The fire was chuckling happily as Honeysuckle opened her book.

She tried to read, but her mind kept straying back to Sergeant Monmouth. Honeysuckle looked up and out of the window. The canal was less icy today and there were two ducks paddling bravely through the chilly water. She breathed on the glass and drew a heart in the mist with her finger. Were her mum and Sergeant Monmouth in love?

This was probably the scariest thought that Honeysuckle could possibly have had – much worse than the thought of ghosts! She couldn't sit still for a moment longer or let this thought stay in her head. She jumped up and put on her music as loud as she dared. She banged her way through into her cabin and began to throw her clothes around while she tried on as many different combinations of her skirts, trousers, jumpers, boots, shoes, tights as she could find. Anything to keep busy and not *think*.

She ended up wearing red tights, black leggings, a huge red and orange striped jumper that hung down almost to her knees, a pink woolly scarf wound round her head (like Rita's, the night before last) and her pair of flower-printed Doc Martens which she had found herself at a jumble sale. 'There!' she said triumphantly, as she pinned on her Dog Walkers' badge along with three other badges and a Christmas tree brooch that flashed.

It was the only thing to do: to be as business-like as possible and just get on with the job in hand. After all, the Dog Walkers' Club was her very own Brilliant Idea and she wasn't going to let some soppy policeman and his stupid stories, and a creepy-looking house mess that up.

'Right!' said Honeysuckle, stuffing the last of her clothes back under her bunk. 'Time to go!'

Her lovely positive mood dissolved when she got out into the open air. The brightness of the day had disappeared; everywhere looked so grey, so cheerless and so misty and spooky.

Honeysuckle walked along with her head lowered.

She thought about what she had seen in the crystal ball. 'It was so horrible,' she muttered softly for about the hundredth time as she turned the corner into The Oaks.

The inside of Number 13 The Oaks was no less terrifying than the outside had been. It was dark and gloomy and the furniture was all old and tatty and there was a smell – a bit like something going mouldy somewhere.

Before she went out, Ms Moribunda showed Honeysuckle where the kitchen was and how to boil the ancient kettle. But the kitchen was down a long, echoing corridor and Honeysuckle didn't much like the thought of venturing in there on her own.

Instead, she sat huddled with Twitter in a room Ms Moribunda had described as 'the snug', although there really wasn't anything at all snug about it. It was small and gloomily lit by one lamp in a corner. The walls were painted mossy green and the furniture was covered in dark brown tapestry-like material. There was no television and the only entertainment she could find was a pack of playing cards. With these she was attempting to play patience while she huddled next to the single bar of an electric heater.

It was no good. She couldn't get warm. Honeysuckle

65

and Twitter were shivering as much as each other. She thought about the ghostly shape she had seen in the crystal ball and that made her shiver even more. Perhaps if I close the door this room might warm up a little, she thought. She crossed to the door and pushed it to. It creaked and slowly opened again. Honeysuckle tried again. This time she pushed the door harder and heard it click shut. But no sooner had she turned to go back to the heater than it creaked slowly open once more.

'Oooh!' wailed Honeysuckle. 'I don't like this!'

Her voice came out much louder than she had expected and poor Twitter, who had been sleeping shakily by her side, leaped to his feet. He stood quivering for a moment before jittering across the room and squeezing himself through the open door.

Where's he gone? wondered Honeysuckle fearfully.

Then she tried to pull herself together. 'I'm sure he'll be back in a minute or two, she thought, there's nothing to worry about . . . I'll just wait here.'

She waited a while but Twitter didn't reappear and all she could hear was a clock ticking in the hall. 'I think I ought to find him,' she said to herself. 'After all, I am meant to be looking after him.'

She got up and crept towards the door. She didn't

really know why she was being so quiet when there was only her and one small dog in the house. But however much she reasoned with herself, she still didn't dare make any noise.

She opened the door of the snug a little wider and stepped out into the hall. She gasped when she looked up at the inside of the front door and saw in the dwindling light two pillars with strange carved creatures sitting on their tops. The creatures had evil, menacing eyes and long claw-like fingers. Honeysuckle shuddered and hugged herself as she turned to walk down the corridor in search of Twitter.

She reached the bottom of a long, curving staircase and craned her neck to see if the dog was on the stairs. She couldn't see him, but she did notice that halfway up the stairs there was a blank space in the wall. It looked like a window frame but it had no window in it; the space had been bricked in. The hair on the back of Honeysuckle's neck stood up – hadn't Sergeant Monmouth said that the merchant had blackened the windows of his house so that no one could see his beautiful wife Harriet Fielding? Perhaps he'd bricked some in as well.

Suddenly she heard a whimper. Where was it coming

from? Honeysuckle crept further down the corridor to the kitchen. She clicked on the light. Although Twitter was nowhere to be seen and the kitchen was dismal, the light made Honeysuckle feel a little braver. She turned to go back down the corridor. 'Ugh!' she squealed as something brushed her cheek. 'What was *that*?' She put her hand up to her face. A cobweb – it was a cobweb, nothing scarier than that! 'Stupid!' she said out loud as she pushed open another door in the corridor.

Honeysuckle stared into the gloom. She couldn't make out anything clearly in the room but she was pretty certain that there was some*one* or some*thing* lurking in the shadows. She swallowed and clicked the light switch down. But nothing happened. She felt her way cautiously to a small table that was not too far from the door. There was a lamp on the table and Honeysuckle fumbled with the switch before managing to turn it on.

As the room lit up, Honeysuckle let out a sigh of relief. The presence she had felt was Twitter; he was here, safe and sound. She moved across the room towards him before noticing that he was shivering and trembling in a way that she hadn't seen him do before. It was as if he could sense that there was something strange in the room. The little dog began to yowl; it was a mournful, blood-chilling sound and Honeysuckle gasped in horror as she realised that he was standing next to a large, brick fireplace.

Chapter Nine

Jaime, Billy and Anita had all felt bad about letting Honeysuckle go to Number 13 The Oaks on her own. As soon as their football match was over, Billy and Jaime went to collect Anita. When Honeysuckle reached the end of The Oaks, having said goodbye to Ms Moribunda, she found them all waiting for her.

'Are you OK?' asked Anita anxiously, as the street-light lit up Honeysuckle's pale face.

'What happened?' asked Jaime. 'You look awful!'

'It was horrible!' said Honeysuckle, and she began to tell them about Twitter quivering next to the fireplace.

'Why was that so awful?' asked Anita. 'Why was Twitter doing that?'

'It was all because—' Honeysuckle began.

'What?' asked the others. 'It was all because what?'

'Because dogs have a sixth sense,' she finished.

'What do you mean?' asked Jaime and Billy together.

'They can sense things that we can't see,' Honeysuckle explained. 'You know – *supernatural* things!'

'Like ghosts, you mean?' asked Billy. 'That's what you mean, isn't it – that Twitter could sense that there was a ghost in the house?'

'Mmmm,' said Honeysuckle. 'I think so.'

'But why would Twitter think there was a ghost in the fireplace?' asked Jaime.

Honeysuckle bit her lip and looked at each of her friends in turn.

'There's something I've got to tell you,' she said, linking arms with Jaime and Anita as they set off towards Billy's house. 'You know I told you that Sergeant Monmouth keeps popping in . . .?'

'Yeah!' said Billy with a smirk. 'He fancies your mum, doesn't he?'

Honeysuckle gawped at him. Did everyone know? She shook her head and tried not to think about that; she had more important things to deal with at the moment. 'Yes, well, whatever . . .' she went on. 'He keeps coming round and telling us long stories about past crimes and all sort of horrible things that have happened in the town . . .'

'And?' asked Jaime.

'And when he heard that we were coming to this area, he told my mum and me this gruesome story about what had happened round here many, many years ago . . .' And that was it. The whole horrifying story about the merchant and his beautiful bride came spilling out. It was a relief really, to tell the others. She hadn't meant to; she was going to keep his story a secret because she had tried to convince herself that it wasn't true, but now . . . now she had evidence! Twitter had sensed a ghost in that house and the ghost was somewhere around the fire-place – exactly the place where poor Harriet Fielding had been hidden by her husband. Number 13 The Oaks *must* have been the mad merchant's own home.

'Wow!' breathed Billy when she had finished. 'What an amazing story!'

'I think it's a really beastly story,' murmured Anita, who was looking very scared. 'I don't like it at all!'

'But listen,' said Honeysuckle, concerned that she had upset her friend, 'maybe Sergeant Monmouth – or Motormouth as I call him – got it wrong . . .' She didn't believe this but she hoped it would comfort Anita to hear it.

'I think we should investigate that fireplace,' said Billy, 'before we jump to conclusions.' He was doing his superhero act, but Honeysuckle wasn't going to have Billy think that he was braver than the girls.

'Well, I've promised Ms Moribunda that we will dog-sit at Number 13 tomorrow,' Honeysuckle told them.

Anita gasped but Jaime and Billy both said, 'Yeah! I'm up for that!' Anita, deciding that she didn't want to be left out, added nervously, 'I'll come too!'

The Fearless Dog Walkers straightened their shoulders and walked on.

'Doesn't Sergeant Motormouth ever tell you any *nice* stories?' Anita asked Honeysuckle in a tiny little voice.

'No,' Honeysuckle answered. 'He only tells us stuff about bikes being stolen and valuable pets going missing and break-ins – stuff like that.'

'Oh, that's a shame!' said Anita.

'Come on, you guys,' said Billy. 'I'll ask my mum to cook us something to eat and then we can plan exactly what we're going to do tomorrow.'

Chapter Ten

'We should have a ghost hunt,' said Billy, when the four of them were happily tucking in to fish and chips cooked by Billy's mum.

Anita gasped with horror.

'Brilliant idea!' said Honeysuckle enthusiastically, and Jaime agreed.

Honeysuckle had to admit that she didn't know what had got into her – but she suspected that what she really wanted to do was to snub Sergeant Monmouth in some way. She wanted to convince herself that she wasn't frightened by his stories. He might have got it all wrong anyway and she wanted proof that her mum's admirer was a complete twit.

'I've read somewhere,' Honeysuckle continued, 'that if you give a ghost a direct command, it will obey you.'

She gave Anita a comforting hug. 'What we have to do is to get the ghost of Harriet Fielding, if that's who it is, to show itself and then command it to leave Number 13 The Oaks and never return!'

'Maybe the ghost of the mad merchant is wandering about as well. We could tell him to get lost too!' Billy suggested.

'Oooooh!' Anita wailed. 'Do we have to? Couldn't we just go and walk some of the nice dogs we know instead of sitting with that creepy, shivery whippet?'

'It'll be fun!' said Jaime, sounding surprisingly brave now that they were well away from The Oaks. 'I've never been on a ghost hunt and you'll be quite safe Anita, I promise you!'

Honeysuckle didn't see for a moment how Jaime could promise that they would be safe but Anita looked a little happier. 'Anyway,' Honeysuckle added, 'we have to take Blossom and Hamlet and that sheepdog called Patch out in the morning – so we'll make loads of money tomorrow – think of that!'

'Mmm,' said Anita doubtfully.

'Let's go back to The Patchwork Snail now, and eat chocolate cake for pudding. Then we'll make a list of what we are going to need for The Ghosthunt,' suggested Honeysuckle.

The others agreed – it was great in Billy's flat and his mum, who was round and cuddly, was really nice, but it made Honeysuckle feel uneasy to be four floors up in the air. She felt much safer on the water; the gentle movement of the houseboat was soothing and she could see trees from the windows, whereas Billy's windows looked out on to other flats.

They all loved being on The Patchwork Snail: it was so different from the sorts of houses and flats that they each lived in. Billy had fantasies about living on a houseboat himself one day and being able to sail off down the canals and rivers whenever he wanted a change of scenery. Anita, Billy and Jaime all had brothers and sisters and they each imagined that being an only child had to be so much nicer.

As Honeysuckle had never known anything different, she didn't know whether the way she lived was better or not. What she did know was that she loved the smell of wood smoke and the puff of warm air that greeted them when she opened the hatch of The Patchwork Snail. She loved the way her little cabin looked so cheerful with its bright painted walls, sparkly cushions and spotty curtains. She loved sharing the tiny space with her mum and she couldn't bear the thought of giving it all up because of some *policeman*. Honeysuckle imagined it would be worse than being in prison to have to live in an ordinary house, especially with *him*.

She felt safe and calm back in the saloon. The boat had lost the creepy feeling that had been there after her strange dreams. Compared to Number 13 The Oaks, Honeysuckle thought it was the cosiest, friendliest place in the world.

She got the chocolate cake out of the tiny larder in the galley and cut it into large slices. Honeysuckle put a slice on each of the four bright blue plates that were usually displayed on a shelf above the cooker and handed them round.

'I'm just going to put the details of today's dog-sit in the registration book,' she said, getting the green book out. 'And then we can begin to plan for tomorrow.'

Maybe it was the warmth of the saloon or the sparkle of fairy lights twinkling out through the little windows of The Patchwork Snail. Or maybe it was the paper chains reminding them all that Christmas was coming. Or perhaps it was just the gooey chocolate cake and the fact that they were all facing something scary together. Whatever it was, when Honeysuckle began to make a list of the things that they might need for their ghost hunt, Anita got gigglier and gigglier. They had all expected her to bottle out, as Billy put it, but as it was, she was becoming quite hysterical with excitement.

'Why don't you bring your digital camera, Billy?' she asked with a huge grin. 'Then you could take photos of the ghosts!'

'Yeah!' agreed Billy. 'That would be awesome.'

Honeysuckle wrote *camera* on the list.

'And we should have reels of thread,' Anita went on, with her cheeks getting pinker and pinker, 'so that we can string it across the rooms and see if any living thing has passed through!'

'That's really clever,' said Honeysuckle, writing *thread* on the list.

'I think I had better bring my dad's blowtorch so that I can exterminate any supernatural beings,' said Billy earnestly.

'Um,' said Honeysuckle with her pencil poised, 'do you think that's a good idea? What if you set fire to Ms Moribunda's curtains or something?'

'Oh, yeah,' Billy said, looking crestfallen. 'I hadn't thought of that.'

'Could you bring an ordinary torch instead?' she suggested.

'Yeah,' said Billy, 'and I could bring my dad's big ther-mometer – then we could detect any drop in the tem-perature.'

'Why would we need to do that?' asked Jaime.

'Because,' Billy replied, 'there is always a drop in tem-perature when there is someone from the other side around!'

'Oh that's brilliant!' screeched Anita. 'I'll bring a bag of flour, just in case.'

No one liked to ask her 'just in case what?' so Honeysuckle wrote down *bag of flour* on the list to keep her happy.

'Should I bring my crystal ball so that we could predict when a ghost is about to appear?' asked Honeysuckle.

'That's a fantastic idea,' Anita gushed. 'This is all going to be SO amazing!'

Honeysuckle, Jaime and Billy were now all seriously worried that Anita might have overdosed on chocolate cake and be having some sort of sugar rush. They exchanged glances and silently agreed that they wouldn't talk about the ghost hunt any more. There was only so much excitement that they felt would be good for Anita.

'So,' said Honeysuckle, folding up the list, 'let's meet

at eleven tomorrow morning, by the clock in the town and collect our first lot of clients for the day. And after their walks, we'll go to Ms Moribunda's . . .'

Chapter Eleven

By the time Rita called her for breakfast, Honeysuckle had already put the things she needed for the ghost hunt into her flowery backpack. She hid the bag under the blankets on her bed and went through into the galley kitchen.

'I thought I heard you up and about.' Rita smiled. 'What's made you such an early bird this morning?'

'Oh,' yawned Honeysuckle, trying to disguise her terrified excitement about the day ahead. 'I just woke up early, that's all. And we've got two jobs today.'

'Honeybunch, that is *so* brilliant. I am proud of you!' squeaked Rita as she rushed at Honeysuckle with her arms wide. She hugged her tightly and gave her a smacking kiss, which made her enormous multi-coloured earrings flash, reflecting the fairy lights.

'Where are the jobs? Whose dogs are you walking?'

Honeysuckle explained what the Dog Walkers had to do that day and how they were going to dog-sit Twitter again in the afternoon.

Rita stood back and looked hard at Honeysuckle. 'So Sergeant Monmouth didn't frighten you then, with his stories?'

'Of course not,' bluffed Honeysuckle. But then, seeing her opportunity, she asked, 'Do you fancy Sergeant Monmouth? Is that why you said you wanted to move to a house?' She felt her cheeks going pink as she watched Rita gulp.

'Blimey!' she said with her purple-eye-lined eyes stretched wide. 'It *has* been fun having someone to go out with and you know I'm always going on about this floating disaster and how hard it is to keep it afloat . . . but as to moving in with him . . . well! Whatever gave you that idea? I think the Sergeant's a bit lonely, that's all – he just wants some company . . . don't you think?'

'Hmm,' Honeysuckle replied.

'Besides,' said Rita as she scooped up her fake fur coat and rammed her arms into the sleeves, 'I haven't got time for any "fancying" – I've got a salon to run and Nev is threatening to leave again so I'll have to be extra specially sweet to him today. What's more, I've got to whizz round with my feather duster before the first customers arrive so I'd better get going!' She kissed Honeysuckle again as she whirled, like a tornado, out through the cabin and up the little steps to the hatch. 'Leave everything shipshape,' she called and then she added, 'I love you, Honeybunch!'

'Aye aye, Captain,' Honeysuckle called back with a big grin. 'Love you too!'

Honeysuckle went on smiling to herself as the hatch banged shut. There was no way that her mum could ever fall for someone like Sergeant Motormouth; she was way too clever for that. Honeysuckle leaned against the sink in the kitchen and poured herself a bowl of Frosties. While she munched her cereal, she thought about the day ahead. She hoped that Anita would be a bit calmer by now and that the walk this morning would help them all work out the finer details of the ghost hunt. She imagined herself at Number 13 The Oaks protecting the others cowering behind her, while she alone confronted the ghost of Harriet Fielding. She would stand firm and demand that it left the house immediately. In her mind she could see the others cheering her incredible bravery and lifting her up on to their shoulders and telling her that she was a star. She would smile graciously at them and tell them that she knew she was blessed with special gifts and that it was her duty to use them well . . .

The Patchwork Snail suddenly lurched in the water as a motor launch came chugging past. Honeysuckle grabbed hold of the sink to steady herself while the boat pitched and dived in the icy black canal. She abandoned her Frosties on the draining board and watched helplessly as they slithered and slopped into the sink.

'Oh sugar!' she growled when the milk from her cereal bowl splashed over the sleeve of her favourite black roll-neck jumper. She had to wait until all the sloshing and sploshing had ebbed away before she could rub the milky stain off with the kitchen cloth. Being buffeted about by passing boats had to be one of the main disadvantages of living on a houseboat, Honeysuckle thought. There really weren't many others. And she set to work tidying the place up before getting ready for the first job of the day.

The walk with Blossom, Hamlet and Patch went smoothly enough. Patch was very energetic and they had to take it in turns to play ball with him. They never worried that he wouldn't come back if they let him off his lead – he always rounded the ball up as if it was a stray lamb and always brought it back to the Dog Walkers and dropped it at their feet. The little Yorkie, Hamlet, enjoyed scrunching through the frosty leaves and even Blossom seemed to be having fun.

They were so busy with the dogs that Honeysuckle, Jaime, Billy and Anita really hadn't time to talk properly about the ghost hunt. When they'd returned the dogs to their owners, Honeysuckle suggested that the best thing to do would be to go to the Moo Bar for a milkshake. They could sit down and check that they had everything ready for the afternoon ahead.

Jaime had thoughtfully brought sandwiches for them all, which they ate on their way, and while they sucked noisily on the straws of their strawberry shakes, Honeysuckle scrabbled about in the bottom of her back-pack and brought out her checklist.

'Billy,' she said, frowning at the list 'have you got your camera?'

'Check, and I brought some rope – I thought that might be useful,' he replied.

'Good thinking,' said Honeysuckle, writing *rope* on

her list. 'And did you bring the torch and the ther-mometer?'

'Check,' said Billy again and Honeysuckle ticked them off her list.

'Great. Did you bring some thread, Anita?' Honeysuckle asked.

Anita opened her mouth as if she was about to say something but only a little squeak came out. Her eyes were huge and she was beginning to look very pale and she definitely wasn't giggly today.

'That's good,' said Honeysuckle in her most matter-of-fact voice. 'I brought some thread as well, just in case, and I've got my crystal ball, my notebook and pencil, so that I can write down sightings, and my watch with the second hand so that I can record the exact times that things happen.'

'Oooh,' moaned Anita, hugging her stomach.

'Here,' said Jaime passing her the rest of her milk-shake, 'have something else to drink – quick!'

Anita's next moan was stifled by a large mouthful of strawberry milkshake.

'Good,' said Honeysuckle, packing her notebook away, 'everything seems to be in order. So – perhaps we'd better go?'

Anita took a last long gurgling suck on the straw of her milkshake and then the Dog Walkers were ready to leave.

Chapter Twelve

On this particular day, Number 13 The Oaks didn't look any less creepy than it had the day before. The weather was a little warmer and the ice was melting, but this made the trees that lined the road drip drearily. Despite the soft winter sun, the street was as gloomy as ever and Number 13 looked depressingly dismal as the Dog Walkers approached the house.

Ms Moribunda already had her coat and hat on when she opened the creaking front door; she looked pale and hollow-eyed as usual.

'I have several appointments with estate agents today,' she said anxiously, 'and I don't expect that I will be back for quite a few hours. There are cakes and tea in the kitchen for you. Twitter is in there, sitting by the heater,' she said, pointing towards the snug.

The heavy front door banged shut behind Ms Moribunda, and Honeysuckle and the others were left standing in the echoing hall. 'I bet she wants to sell this place because it's haunted – that's why she's going to see estate agents,' said Billy. He was staring up at the creepy creatures on the pillars each side of the door. Anita followed his gaze and clamped her hand over her mouth in horror. Honeysuckle and Jaime both agreed that Billy was probably right but Anita didn't make a sound. She hadn't said a word since they left the Moo Bar and now her teeth were chattering badly.

'Come on,' said Honeysuckle, firmly taking Anita's arm. 'Let's go and find Twitter.' They walked into the gloomy snug and gathered themselves around the radiator and the little dog. He looked pleased to see them and wagged his skinny tail approvingly. Jaime gave him a big hug and for a moment he stopped quivering. 'Are we going to begin straight away? We've got everything, haven't we, so why don't we set it all up?' she asked the others.

'Good idea,' said Billy, jumping to his feet. 'I vote we leave Twitter in here while we set the ghost traps in the hallway and around the door of the panelled room with the fireplace.'

'I think you're right,' agreed Honeysuckle. 'We shouldn't waste any time. And we don't want Twitter to set off the traps by mistake.' She looked at Anita who was beginning to go a bit green. 'Would you like to look after Twitter in here?' she asked her. 'It would be a really important job, making sure that he's OK.'

'Mmm.' Anita nodded. She looked wide-eyed at the others. 'What are you going to do first?' she asked in a trembling voice.

Honeysuckle squatted down between her and the radiator. 'I think we'll put the threads across the corridor first and station Billy by the staircase with his camera ... Jaime and I will stay in the kitchen with the thermometer and keep watch.' She glanced at Jaime who nodded bravely. 'I will be monitoring any changes in temperature, you keep an eye on Twitter and report ... ewww ...' She paused, sniffing the air. 'What's that horrible, sour smell?'

'Is is a ghost?' squeaked Anita, nearly jumping out of her skin.

'I don't know,' said Honeysuckle. 'Can you smell it?'

Jaime sniffed around like a tracker dog. She bent down towards Honeysuckle and said, 'Actually, I think it's coming from you!'

'Wha—?' squealed Honeysuckle, giving her jumper a good sniff. 'Eww! You're right!' She giggled. 'It's the milk that splashed me this morning! I can't have washed it off properly!' She laughed again and even Anita managed a wan little smile. 'I'll give it another scrub when we get into the kitchen. Come on, guys, I think we'd better get started.'

Anita handed the bag of flour to Jaime, which was her contribution to the hunt. 'This could be really useful – if there is a presence we could sprinkle it with flour to make it more visible.' Honeysuckle didn't really see how that would work but she didn't want Anita to be any more upset than she already was, so she said nothing.

They left Anita in the snug and began to explore the ground floor. First they went to the end of the dark corridor that led from the front door to the back of the house. The floorboards creaked dreadfully and any whispers they uttered echoed round the walls. They crept into the kitchen, which was tucked under the dark oak staircase. It was no brighter than the rest of the house but it was a little warmer. There was an old range cooker along the back wall giving out a little heat. In the middle of the room was a small wooden table with a yellowy-brown cloth over it. The tea things and cakes were set out on the shabby table. There was a door with frosted glass that led from the kitchen out into a for-lorn, overgrown garden at the back of the house. Jaime turned the key in the lock and tried to open the door thinking that they could put Twitter out later. It opened too little and then stuck – she had to tug hard to make it open properly. It finally swung wide and Jamie shud-dered when she saw the thicket of brambles and under-growth that was threatening to push its way into the kitchen. She pushed the door shut again as Billy said, 'I think we should take off our shoes – we need to be as quiet as possible.' Jaime and Honeysuckle agreed and they left their shoes and trainers by the cooker.

'Let's start by putting the threads across the hall – do you think we should check upstairs first?' asked Billy.

'You go and we'll keep watch down here,' suggested Honeysuckle.

Billy set off with his torch but he didn't get very far. When he reached the bottom of the stairs, he put his foot on the first step, which creaked loudly, echoing through the silence of the house. 'Woaaah . . .!' He stepped back immediately but not before Anita's ashen face had peered round the door of the snug. Billy cleared his throat. 'Perhaps I'll just take a few photos of the staircase instead.' He took his camera out of his pocket and began snapping away at the dark corners of the staircase and hall. 'Right, that's done,' he whispered and smiled reassuringly at Anita who crept back behind the door.

Billy, Jaime and Honeysuckle spent a long time attaching threads across the doorway into the haunted room and down the corridor. It was difficult because they didn't dare put the lights on. They all felt that they had to work in the dwindling light so that the atmosphere was right for spirits.

When they had finished, Billy positioned himself with his camera at the bottom of the stairs, facing the front door and with a good view of the other doorways. Jaime and Honeysuckle crouched together in the kitchen with the thermometer and waited . . . and waited . . . and waited . . . and began to get bored.

'I've got a couple of apples,' whispered Jaime. 'Do you want one?' Honeysuckle nodded and Jaime produced a plastic bag with two apples in it. She handed one to Honeysuckle and began munching on the other one.

As they were nibbling the last little bits of fruit and beginning to think that this ghost hunt was a waste of time, Billy suddenly hissed, 'Can you hear that?'

Jaime and Honeysuckle stopped chewing and strained their ears. There was a faint but distinct scratching sound. Jaime stared wide-eyed at Honeysuckle, who stared back at her. Then there was a scuttling noise. 'Quick! There's something coming!' hissed Billy.

Jaime leaped up, yanked open the back door and threw the apple cores out. Then she peered down the corridor while Billy clicked furiously on his camera. Neither of them could *see* anything but they could all *hear* it . . . a sound like little footsteps! Honeysuckle stepped out from under the stairs with the thermometer in her hand. 'Eeeek!' she squealed, 'the temperature's dropping!'

'And look,' said Billy, pointing his camera into the gloom. 'Look there! That white thing on the floor! It wasn't there before – it's . . . it's ECTOPLASM!!'

'Oooooh!' wailed Jaime, 'and there's a terrible smell – like rotting flesh!'

Honeysuckle could smell it too and it wasn't her milk-stained jumper this time. 'What's happening?' she wailed as the air around her grew colder and colder.

'I don't know.' Jaime shuddered and then suddenly everything changed.

There was a crashing noise and at that very moment

Anita stepped into the hall and switched the lights on.

'Oh!' Honeysuckle, Jaime and Billy all said in turn.

Honeysuckle said, 'Oh!' because she realised that the bang she had just heard was the back door hitting the kitchen wall. The drop in temperature had nothing to do with a wandering spirit – Jaime must have left the door open when she threw out the apple cores.

Billy then said 'Oh!' because he could now see that his ectoplasm was only the white plastic bag that the apples had been in. Disappointingly, it was not moving on its own but was being blown by the draught from the kitchen door.

Jaime said 'Oh!' next, because, as she ran to close the back door, she realised that the terrible stench of death was in fact Billy's trainers, which were cooking slightly in the warmth from the cooker.

'What's going on?' asked Anita, shakily, looking at them each in turn.

Honeysuckle looked shyly at her. 'Um . . . nothing much.' Then she stopped and, putting up her hand to signal that no one should move, she whispered, 'Except that!' And then all four Dog Walkers heard the unmistakable sound of wailing.

Chapter Thirteen

Anita clutched Billy, who happened to be closest to her. 'What was that?' she rasped, squeezing his arm hard.

'Dunno,' said Billy, trying to prise her fingers off, as his arm was beginning to hurt.

'Shhh!' demanded Honeysuckle.

They all listened closely again. And there it was! Not only the pathetic sound of wailing but also the sound of long, uncared for nails scratching and scrabbling.

'Where's it coming from?' asked Jaime.

'The panelled room!' breathed Honeysuckle. 'We're going to have to go in and investigate!'

'No!' squealed Anita. 'We can't go in – we mustn't go in – it's *haunted*!'

'Well, that's the whole point!' Billy said, rather

sarcastically. 'We're here to find a ghost and that's where it is, in there!'

'It must be the ghost of Harriet Fielding,' whispered Honeysuckle, feeling more and more certain. 'She's crying and scratching and desperate to be set free . . .'

'Set free?' gasped Anita. 'You're not going to let it out, are you?'

'We have to let her ghost out,' explained Honeysuckle, 'so that we can tell it to leave.'

'Can't we tell it from here?' Anita asked, with her face scrunched into an agonised expression.

'No, that won't work – she, or rather her ghost, has to be out and about before we can give it a direct command,' whispered Honeysuckle.

'Out and about?' Anita gaped incredulously. And then, finding some courage, she whispered, 'What if it isn't Harriet Fielding? What if it's someone else – someone who's got in there by mistake? Couldn't you check in your crystal ball? It might at least tell us who it is in there making that scary noise!'

The others looked at her in astonishment.

'That's a really good idea,' hissed Jaime. 'Go on, Honeysuckle, look in your crystal ball and check that it is who we think it is.'

Honeysuckle agreed and went back into the snug to find her backpack; the others followed. As she drew the velvet-covered crystal ball from her bag with trembling fingers, Billy, Anita and Jaime gathered closely around her.

'You mustn't get too close,' she said, waving them back. 'I need space and I have to concentrate. She popped the ball on to its little wooden stand and began to gaze into its shining centre. So far, she could see a smeary smudge on the surface of the ball, but nothing more. There wasn't a sound other than the ticking of the clock in the hallway. They were too far from the panelled room to hear any crying or scratching. Honeysuckle pressed her nose closer to the ball. She *must* be able to see something. She suddenly gasped.

'What? What is it? What can you see?' the others asked, straining to look into the secret depths of the crystal ball.

Honeysuckle leaned back. 'It's gone!' she said.

'What? What's gone?' begged Jaime. 'What did you see?'

'I saw,' Honeysuckle said slowly, 'I saw a strange, grey, fuzzy shape . . . just like I saw before . . . it looked . . . sad . . . I think it was the shape of . . .'

'Harriet Fielding!' Anita finished the sentence for her.

'Yes, it must have been the shape of Harriet Fielding's ghost . . .'

'Which means,' said Billy, 'that we have to go into that panelled room and *liberate* it!'

'We could take Twitter with us this time,' said Jaime. 'He can be our ghost detector.'

'We don't really need a detector as we know that the ghost is already there but it would be good to have him, just in case there's more than one ghost . . .' Honeysuckle trailed off as she could see the tears welling up in Anita's eyes. 'It'll be all right,' she said, as reassuringly as she could. 'You can stay in here if you like.'

'I'm not going to stay in here on my own. What if a ghost came and you were all next door? N-n-n-no . . .' she stammered, 'I'm coming with you!'

'Billy, why don't you give Anita the torch? Then she can put it on if she gets scared,' Honeysuckle said as she put her precious crystal ball back in its velvet pouch. Billy handed the torch to Anita and they all tiptoed towards the hallway. Anita stuck close to Honeysuckle's shoulder. She was breathing heavily but, when Billy broke through the threads and opened the door of the panelled room, she held her breath until Honeysuckle got so worried that she had to prod her in the tummy.

'Phew!' Anita let out a gasp of air.

'Shhh!' Jaime hissed, and they all stopped, statue still, and listened.

There it was again! That pathetic, sad, wailing sound and the scratching . . . Twitter began to tremble in Billy's arms. He put the little dog down. Twitter went straight towards the fireplace and stood quivering and shaking just as he had before, but this time he whined a little as well.

'That's her!' whispered Honeysuckle. 'We've got to set her ghost free!'

'How are we going to do that?' asked Jaime, while Anita began to shake almost as much as the dog.

'We'll have to go over there – to the fireplace,' said Billy, 'and work out exactly where she is.'

'Yes,' said Honeysuckle. 'You go first then.' She pushed Billy towards the other side of the room. 'Go on!'

Billy tiptoed across the creaking wooden floorboards and the others tiptoed behind him – first Honeysuckle, then Jaime and finally Anita. She had her eyes tight shut and was hanging on to the strap of Jaime's dungarees to stop herself from falling over. When Billy stopped suddenly, Anita crashed into Jaime and almost sent her flying.

'Shhh!' Billy hissed again as they gathered round the fireplace. They listened again. The sounds were louder now and Twitter was quaking violently.

'You see?' whispered Honeysuckle. 'He knows exactly where the ghost is!'

Billy had stepped forward fearlessly. 'Come and shine the torch over here, Anita,' he said, but Anita couldn't move. She reached out towards Billy and with a trembling hand she gave the torch back to him. Billy was peering up the chimney through the gloom. 'I'm very close to her!' he whispered, switching the torch on. 'But I can't see a way of letting her out.' Just then the light from the torch flickered and died. 'Damn,' said Billy, shaking the torch and trying the switch again.

Not wanting to be outdone by a boy, Honeysuckle went right up to the chimney-breast and put her ear to it. She put her hand over her mouth and with her eyes impossibly round her muffled voice said, 'She's in here!' She ran her hands over the brickwork. 'There isn't any way in,' she whispered as the wailing grew more and more plaintive.

Billy ducked his head out of the chimney. 'I can't see how on earth we're going to liberate her ghost . . .'

'I could climb up the chimney,' Jaime volunteered.

'No, no – wait a minute!' spluttered Honeysuckle. 'I think I might have had a Brilliant Idea!

Chapter Fourteen

'As there is no way of liberating the ghost from the inside,' Honeysuckle said quietly, 'let's go and investigate the chimney from the *outside*! I bet there's a way we could liberate Harriet Fielding's ghost into the garden!'

Anita groaned softly and buried her face in her hands.

'That *is* a brilliant idea. Come on, you guys, let's go and see,' whispered Jamie, enthusiastically, and she bounded back across the panelled room with Billy behind her.

'I'll bring my rope,' he said. 'Never know, it might be useful.'

'OK,' said Honeysuckle, dragging Anita out into the corridor. 'Do you want to stay here while we go?' she whispered into her friend's ear.

'Nooooo!' Anita gave a small, strangled cry. 'I'm coming with you!'

'Good!' Honeysuckle gave her hand a little squeeze and moved purposefully towards the back door.

'Have you got the torch?' Anita asked in a tiny, quavering voice.

'Yup!' Billy replied, giving the torch a good shake; it flickered on and then off again. 'I think it's had it though,' he said gloomily.

'It's all right,' said Honeysuckle. 'It's not quite dark yet and I'm sure we'll be able to find our way.'

Billy and Jaime had put on their shoes and were already standing in the open back doorway. Billy beckoned to Honeysuckle and Anita to hurry up and the four Dog Walkers were soon crowding together looking out into the brambly confusion of Ms Moribunda's garden. Twitter, who had been trembling like a leaf on the doorstep, suddenly flashed through their legs and into the thicket.

'Where's he gone?' asked Jaime anxiously. She began to try and kick her way past a large bramble bush.

'I bet he's gone to where the ghost is!' replied Billy. 'Come on, we've got to follow him!'

Now that wasn't quite as easy as Billy had hoped. Twitter knew his way round the terrible tangle of brambles and bushes in his owner's garden and he was also very small. To make matters just that little bit more difficult, there was really only a smudge of light left in the leaden afternoon sky. 'You lead the way, Billy,' said Honeysuckle. 'We'll follow you.'

Billy leaped forward in the direction that Twitter had gone. 'Aargh!' he screeched as the bush he had plunged into folded around him. Just before he disappeared from sight, Honeysuckle was able to catch hold of the rope he had slung over his shoulder and pull him back. 'Ow!' he gasped as his face reappeared from the bush. 'That's prickly!'

'OK, there must be a way round this bush . . . look!' whispered Honeysuckle. 'We could crawl through this gap next to the kitchen wall.' She began to shuffle on her hands and knees under the prickling branches of the bush, keeping her right shoulder close to the wall of the house.

'Follow me!' she commanded. 'We'll be through in a mo – oh yuck . . . what's that?' There was something slimy under her left hand. Oh please, she thought as she lifted her hand up to her nose, don't let this be something that Twitter has done . . . She sniffed – no – it wasn't *that*, but it was something pretty slimy, although she couldn't tell what, exactly. The others were pushing her along from behind so she carried on bravely after wiping her hand on the wall to try and get the slime off.

She began to shiver. It was terrifying fumbling about in the dark, never knowing whether a ghost might appear at any moment. She knew she mustn't let the others know how spooked she felt, but she couldn't help letting out a little scream when a startled bird flapped up in front of her.

'Where are we now?' Anita whimpered as they all emerged in a small clearing.

'I'm sure we must be nearly there,' Honeysuckle said. She suggested that they stay as close to the wall of the house as possible. That way they had to reach the chimney of the panelled room sooner or later.

They took a few more fumbling steps with Jaime leading the way this time. 'Aaaargh!' there was a sudden terrified cry from Anita at the back. 'Something's got me! Something's hanging on to my sweatshirt and won't let me go . . . I think it's a ghost . . . Aaaaargh!'

Honeysuckle spun around shouting, 'Get away from here, you evil spirit!'

'It's no good,' wailed Anita. 'It won't let go . . .' She was sobbing now and Honeysuckle had to fight her way back through prickly undergrowth to reach her. She grabbed hold of her hand and pulled. 'I'm stuck!' cried Anita. 'Help me!'

Honeysuckle peered into the blackness of the bushes; she would have to confront the ghost again. 'Let go of my friend,' she demanded as a little ray of early evening moonlight shone on to Anita. Then suddenly she giggled. 'You nincompoop! You're stuck on a bramble bush, that's all – you're not being held captive by an evil spirit at all!'

'This is hopeless,' said Anita dismally.

'No, it isn't,' Jaime snapped. 'Listen!'

Somewhere, not very far from where they were standing, Twitter was making little whining noises. 'He must have found the ghost!' gasped Honeysuckle. 'We must be nearly there!'

'I think he's just along this wall a bit,' said Jaime. 'Why don't we join hands and try and follow the wall all together.' Everyone liked this idea, so the four brave and intrepid Dog Walkers (well, three, since Anita wasn't feeling at all brave) formed a human chain and shuffled their way towards the sound of Twitter whining.

'There he is!' exclaimed Honeysuckle. She could just see the outline of the little pale dog in the moonlight. 'That must be where the back of the chimney is!'

'And the ghost,' added Jaime. They kept their hands clasped as they took the final steps towards the haunted place.

Now that they were close enough, they could hear the crying, scratching sounds quite clearly. 'Oooh!' said Anita. 'I don't like this!'

'Don't worry,' said Billy, gruffly clutching the useless torch in one hand. 'I've got my rope . . .' What he would do with his rope wasn't at all clear but Anita didn't make any other sound as they surrounded Twitter. They stood motionless, hand in hand, and gazed into the gloom.

'Do you know something?' Honeysuckle whispered, letting go of Jaime and Anita's hands. 'If you listen carefully, you'll hear this ghost isn't wailing . . .' She leaned down, and saw that there was a slab of rendering partly covering a small hole, which looked as if it had recently fallen off the wall. Honeysuckle pushed the rendering away and put her hand into the space and touched ash – it must be the fireplace in the panelled room. Then she felt something soft and furry. Honeysuckle turned and grinned at her friends. 'It isn't *wailing*,' she said, 'it's *meowing*! This ghost isn't a ghost at all – it's a cat!'

'WHAT?' Jaime, Billy and Anita all demanded at once.

'Look,' said Honeysuckle, gently pulling out a sooty cat, as the others gathered round and peered at it.

Chapter Fifteen

When Rita arrived back at The Patchwork Snail that evening, she found the four members of the Dog Walkers' Club squished together on the velvet bench seat singing 'Dancing Queen' at the top of their voices. The glitter of the fairy lights lit up their delighted faces and the houseboat rocked to Abba's rhythm.

'Babes!' Rita shouted above the din. 'Is this a party? Can I join in?' She didn't wait for a reply before she began shimmying and shaking in the galley kitchen. She shrugged off her fake fur coat and flung it through into Honeysuckle's cabin. She had at least four sparkly necklaces on and the beads flashed and sparked like fireworks as she danced around.

'What's going on?' she asked breathlessly after the fourth verse. The Dog Walkers stopped singing and

Honeysuckle grinned at her mum.

'We've been on a ghost hunt!' she said triumphantly.

'Oh babes!' Rita said suddenly looking very serious. 'What do you mean? You haven't been doing anything silly, have you?' The others quietened down and sat very still while Rita frowned at them. 'Tell me everything!' she said sternly.

'It's all right, Mum, honestly,' explained Honeysuckle. 'We were at Number 13 The Oaks . . .'

'That's in the part of town that the Sergeant told us that dreadful story about, isn't it?' asked Rita.

'Yes,' replied Honeysuckle before adding urgently, 'and we thought that Number 13 must have been the merchant's house because we heard all this crying and scratching coming from a wall. But we were wrong! The house isn't haunted at all! And I bet Sergeant Monmouth made all that stuff up just to scare us!'

'Go on,' said Rita, perching herself on the tiny fold-down table opposite the velvet bench seat. She drummed her fingers and waited.

'Well,' Honeysuckle began, 'it all started with Twitter . . .' And she went on to explain to Rita that they thought Twitter had sensed a ghostly presence at Number 13 The Oaks because he trembled and twitched

116

so much. Then she explained how they had heard scratching and crying and had naturally assumed that it was the ghost of Harriet Fielding that they could hear.

'Oh my goodness!' gasped Rita. 'That daft man shouldn't have put all those ideas in your head – so what did you do?'

'We decided that we had to find the ghost and give it a direct command – tell it to leave,' explained Billy.

'Yes,' said Anita, 'because poor Ms Moribunda looked so *haunted* that we knew we had to do something!'

'But it wasn't a ghost!' Honeysuckle grinned. 'It was a cat! And it turned out to be Mrs Pomfrey's priceless pedigree Persian!' She didn't mention the bit about looking in her crystal ball and luckily none of the others did either.

'Good grief,' said Rita. 'Then why was Twitter trembling? What had he sensed?'

'Nothing,' said Honeysuckle. 'Well, that is, nothing *supernatural* – he knew that the sounds we could hear were coming from a cat, not a ghost. And anyway, whippets always tremble.'

'Do they?' asked Rita.

'Yup!' replied Honeysuckle. 'When Ms Moribunda came back, she told us that whippets tremble when they are hot, cold, excited, hungry, tired, cross – in fact, they tremble most of the time and not necessarily because they are frightened or sensing anything creepy!'

Jaime went on, 'Twitter was trembling with excitement because he knew there was a cat nearby and he wanted to chase it!'

'Ha!' laughed Rita, and then she paused. 'So why did Ms Moribunda look so "haunted" as you say?'

'Ms Moribunda looks haunted because she is so worried about the state of her house. We thought she wanted to sell it because of the ghost,' explained Anita.

'That's right,' Honeysuckle continued, 'but it's nothing to do with a ghost at all! She told us she wants to sell Number 13 because there are loads of repairs that need to be done and she doesn't know how she is going to pay for them.'

'Poor woman!' said Rita, and Honeysuckle could see that she was thinking about her own struggle to keep The Patchwork Snail repaired.

'That's why she was out for so long this afternoon – she had to go and see more estate agents and she had to go to the bank to try and borrow some money to make the house smart enough to sell. Then she went to somewhere called the Environmental Health Agency . . .'

'Yeah!' said Billy. 'Ms Moribunda told us that she had a family of squirrels living under her bedroom floor – they were making the footstep noises that we heard, do you remember?' he asked, looking around at the others. 'She said that she had to get this special bloke in to get rid of them!'

'Squirrels!' said Rita. 'My word! What happened to the cat, where did you find it?'

'It was stuck at the back of Ms Moribunda's chimney, a bit of the wall had fallen down and trapped it,' said Honeysuckle

'The chimney?' asked Rita incredulously. 'Just where Sergeant Monmouth told us that poor woman had been bricked up?'

'Exactly,' said Honeysuckle, 'but that was all rubbish. We had to lift it out very carefully; the poor thing was quite thin.'

'And then what did you do with it?' asked Rita.

'Well,' said Jaime, 'when Ms Moribunda came back and we had explained everything to her . . .'

'But not about the ghost hunt, obviously,' Anita put in.

'No, no, we didn't say anything about ghosts,' Jaime agreed. 'She gave us some cold chicken to give the cat and a box so that we could take it to the police station.'

'And that's what we did!' said Honeysuckle happily. 'We took the cat to the police station and they told us that it was definitely Mrs Pomfrey's priceless pedigree Persian and that there was a reward for finding it!'

'Well, well!' said Rita clapping her hands together. 'This does call for a celebration, Honeybunch!' she said, turning to Honeysuckle. 'There's a box of crackers and party poppers under the pile of clothes in my cabin – go and get those and I will make everyone hot chocolate and we can eat some of the mince pies Mrs Whitely-Grub gave me this morning!'

Honeysuckle bounced off into Rita's cabin with Anita following closely behind. When they were through the door, Anita grabbed Honeysuckle's arm and whispered urgently, 'What did you see in the crystal ball then? What was it if it wasn't a ghost?'

Honeysuckle chuckled. 'I should have realised that it wasn't a ghost,' she whispered back. 'I wanted it to be a ghost because that would have made sense but in fact . . .'

'Yes?' said Anita.

'In fact,' Honeysuckle went on, 'the grey, fuzzy shape that I saw had little sharp pointy ears – it was a cat!

That's what I saw in the crystal ball: a cat!'

Anita giggled and her eyes were shining. 'So you do have real fortune-telling powers, don't you?' she said.

Honeysuckle hugged her and together they found the crackers and the party poppers and went back into the saloon.

Chapter Sixteen

'How do I look, Honeybunch?' Rita asked the following morning. She was standing in the saloon with one hand on her hip and the other curved over her head like a ballerina. She wore gold and pink from head to toe with a splash of red here and there. Pink top, gold lacy skirt, pink and red striped tights and her favourite gold ballroom dancing shoes. She had finished the look off with a glittery red ribbon tied round her head and a pair of enormous red and gold earrings.

'Fab!' said Honeysuckle. 'Don't worry about the mess,' she added as she watched Rita look unhappily at the state of the saloon. 'I'll clear it up after you've gone.'

'You are such a doll,' said Rita, blowing her a kiss from the doorway of her cabin. 'We had some fun, didn't we?' she asked.

'Yeah,' said Honeysuckle, as she began to pick up the little frizzled pieces of coloured paper from the party poppers.

'I can tell you I was gasping for a ciggie by the end of it though . . .'

'Mum, you didn't, did you?'

'Certainly not, Honeybunch! I know I've had one or two little slips recently when the demon weed got the better of me, but I promise that I won't be smoking any more. Now, where's that special gum gone? Better take that to work, just in case I'm tempted . . .'

Honeysuckle found the little pack and gave it to her mum. Rita threw it and various other bits and bobs into her huge leopard-print shoulder bag. 'Oh!' she said, slinging the bag over her arm. 'I almost forgot – I want you to come into the salon today; there's something I need to give you. I forgot to bring it home!' However much Honeysuckle pressed her, Rita would not explain why she wanted Honeysuckle at the salon. 'Wait and see!' was all she would say.

'I have to walk Patch and Pudding with the others first,' Honeysuckle said. 'So I won't be there until about two o'clock.'

'That's fine, babes – leave everything shipshape when

you go, won't you?' she called from the top of the steps by Honeysuckle's cabin.

'Aye aye, Captain,' Honeysuckle replied and then she was alone.

While the kettle boiled, Honeysuckle did her best to pick up all the rubbish scattered across the floor from the night before. In amongst the scrumpled bits of paper and jokes from the crackers she found a few small silver stars, which she put carefully on the sideboard.

Although the morning was still dark and gloomy, Honeysuckle felt wonderfully happy and she was certainly confident enough to risk reading the tea-leaves. After all, they were hardly going to show her that she was going to see a ghost today! She followed her usual ritual with the tea and peeped into the bottom of the cup. 'Now, what on earth is that?' Honeysuckle wondered, turning the cup this way and that. If only she was better at understanding what the signs meant! This shape looked like a box, but what did a picture of a box mean? Was it a present? Or . . . was it a coffin? 'No, no,' Honeysuckle scolded herself, 'don't start that again. Of course it's not a coffin! Perhaps it's a sign to tell me that I should get on and buy my Christmas presents . . .'

Whatever it was, Honeysuckle was pretty certain that

it wasn't anything scary. She felt from her head to the tips of her toes that this was going to be a good day. She washed and dressed in sparkly tights, bright blue cut offs, her red and orange striped jumper and her Doc Martens. She found the little silver stars and using a tiny blob of Rita's false eyelash glue (which she was sure Rita wouldn't notice) she stuck the stars on to her cheek. Then she found her favourite homemade tinsel and bead tiara and plonked it on to her head threading it through her thick, black, curling hair.

When she was well wrapped up in her yellow duffle coat and long black scarf, Honeysuckle set off to meet the others. She wondered fleetingly, as she passed her house, why Mrs Whitely-Grub hadn't asked them to take Cupid out for a couple of days. But then she was too busy collecting Pudding and meeting the others to think much more about that.

Pudding was being particularly slow and Patch was particularly energetic, which made it difficult for the Dog Walkers to spend much of their walk all together. One of them had to be dragging along with Pudding while the others played frantic games with Patch. They did, however, have time to wonder what sort of reward there would be for finding Mrs Pomfrey's priceless

Persian cat and exactly how and when they were going to get whatever it was.

'I bet it'll be a picture of a Persian cat,' said Jaime, 'or perhaps some tickets to a cat show!'

'Maybe it'll be tickets to go and see the musical show *Cats*,' said Anita.

'Or a safari trip to see the big cats,' Honeysuckle suggested, 'where we will stay in one of those little huts on stilts and watch animals mooching about underneath . . . and then during the night there will be huge, hairy snakes, which will wrap their bodies round our feet and we will scream and scream until some gorgeous superhero comes to rescue us!'

'What?' asked Anita laughing. 'Why will the snakes be hairy and how come a gorgeous superhero is going to be there?'

'I saw it all in my crystal ball,' Honeysuckle lied as she looked deep into Anita's eyes. 'I have very special powers you know . . . I see that you are going to have sausage and mash for supper and that you will fall in love with a handsome pirate . . .'

'Shut up!' Anita hiccupped. 'You're talking rubbish!'

Honeysuckle laughed and then Billy said, 'She might give us a cat-o'-nine-tails as a reward.'

'A what?' asked Honeysuckle.

'It's a gruesome sort of whip!' said Billy, rubbing his hands together. 'One with nine different strands, for maximum nastiness . . .'

'Stop it, Billy,' said Jaime. 'We've had enough scary stuff to last us for months.'

'Or it could be a massive *cat*apult,' Billy went on and Jaime had to tickle him to make him shut up.

'Whatever it is, we'll share it, won't we?' said Honeysuckle and everyone agreed.

Later, when she had left her friends at the Moo Bar, Honeysuckle went to see her mum in the Curl Up and Dye salon. As she arrived Nev, the assistant, flounced past her and out of the door. Rita came running after him. 'Oh for goodness' sake!' she puffed. 'Don't tell me he's walked out *again*? And all because I asked him to sweep some hair up off the floor. Aargh – what am I going to do with him, Honeybunch? It's enough to send a saint to the ciggies.'

'Mum?' Honeysuckle said with a frown.

'No, no, it's all right, babes – I haven't and I won't, I promise . . . Now, come with me, I've got something for you!'

Honeysuckle followed her mum across the busy salon

to the back room. The whole place was a flurry of activity with hairdryers going left, right and centre. There were people having perms and blow-dries and cuts and trims and colours and streaks and extensions – the noise was amazing. Honeysuckle always wondered how her mum stayed sane.

'Here we are!' Rita said, reaching into a drawer in her office desk. 'This is for you!' She pulled out the most beautiful pale blue leather jewellery box that Honeysuckle had ever seen. She opened her mouth wide and gasped.

'It's from Mrs Whitely-Grub,' Rita explained. 'She went off to Scotland yesterday with the Major and she wanted you to have this as a Christmas present and a thank you for all you have done for her and Cupid!'

'Oh,' said Honeysuckle, 'this is so beautiful . . .' She opened the small silver clasp and gazed at the soft, cream-coloured suede that lined the box. There were places for rings, bracelets and necklaces and all sorts of other useful compartments.

Honeysuckle closed the box again and noticed for the first time that the initials HSFL were engraved on the left-hand corner of the lid. 'Honeysuckle Sabrina Florette Lovelace,' she breathed, running her finger over the letters. This was the box that she had seen in her tea-leaves! This was another prediction that she had almost absolutely and completely got right! 'But what about the others?' she asked anxiously. 'They've all helped look after Cupid as well.'

'Exactly,' agreed Rita. 'Mrs Whitely-Grub left an envelope for each of them,' and she handed Honeysuckle three pale blue envelopes. 'I think it might be a little money.'

Honeysuckle couldn't believe it – she had been singled out for a special present, and after all the bad things she had thought about Mrs Whitely-Grub in the past!

'Oh, and another thing,' Rita went on. 'Sergeant Monmouth dropped in here this morning.'

Honeysuckle frowned.

'It was just to say,' Rita said firmly, glaring at her, 'that Mrs Pomfrey is absolutely delighted to have her cat back and that there is a cheque waiting for you all down at the station.'

Chapter Seventeen

There are many strange things in life. Some things are odd or funny, while others are just plain spooky. What happened next was definitely spooky.

Honeysuckle raced back to the Moo Bar to give Jaime, Billy and Anita their thank you presents from Mrs Whitley-Grub and to tell them about the reward at the police station. Only Jaime was able to go with her to collect the reward as Billy had to go home and Anita was meeting her mum on the other side of town.

The two girls walked together through the darkening afternoon. They met Hamlet and his owner, Mrs Dooley, in the bustling High Street and stopped for a chat. Mrs Dooley booked the Dog Walkers for the following day – there was nothing spooky about that.

When they reached the police station, Honeysuckle and Jaime had to queue up at the front desk before they could talk to the officer in charge. After several minutes it was their turn and Honeysuckle explained who she was and why they were there. The officer said, 'Yes, of course! Mrs Pomfrey's famous pet – you saved us a lot of work by finding that cat and that's for sure. We've just got to fill in the details in the logbook and then I can give you the envelope.' He duly filled in all the information he needed and went off to find the reward – there was nothing spooky about that either.

The officer returned a few moments later with a sealed envelope addressed to *The Dog Walkers*. Honeysuckle took the envelope and signed the logbook to prove that she had received it. They didn't open the envelope there and then; they decided instead to go back to The Patchwork Snail.

'Go on, open it!' said Jaime once they were safely on board with a cup of tea and a chocolate biscuit each. Honeysuckle tore open the envelope and pulled out a sheet of folded pink paper. A cheque fell out from the fold and both Honeysuckle and Jaime gasped when they saw how much money Mrs Pomfrey had given them. That was fantastic, not spooky.

'Wow! How awesome!' said Jaime. 'All that money just for finding a cat!'

'Well,' said Honeysuckle, 'we were amazingly brave and courageous, especially as we thought it was a ghost we were hunting and not a cat at all!' She looked at the cheque again and did some counting on her fingers. 'Even shared between us there is still loads of money each,' she said happily, thinking that she would be able to give Rita lots for The Patchwork Snail Repair Fund.

'Do you think we should give Ms Moribunda some of the money?' asked Jaime. 'After all, the cat was in her chimney . . .'

'I've been thinking about that,' said Honeysuckle, absent-mindedly unfolding Mrs Pomfrey's pink letter. 'What I think we should do is to help her with some of the repairs – you know, so that she can sell Number 13 The Oaks. I've done loads of stuff around here with Mum so it wouldn't be a problem.'

'Yeah!' said Jaime, as Honeysuckle looked down at the letter in her lap. 'That's a wicked idea, I love doing carpentry and . . . Hey! What's the matter?' she asked, seeing Honeysuckle's face turn whiter than snow.

'It's this . . . this letter,' said Honeysuckle shakily.

'Why?' Jaime asked, straining to see what Honeysuckle was looking at. 'What does it say?'

Honeysuckle replied, swallowing hard. 'Well, not only does Mrs Pomfrey live in *'Fielding* House . . .' She looked up at Jaime. 'But also . . . her priceless pedigree Persian cat is called . . . HARRIET!'

Now that was spooky!

Chapter Eighteen

Later that evening, when Honeysuckle had begun to get over the shock of the spooky coincidences in Mrs Pomfrey's letter, she snuggled down with Rita under their hand-knitted multi-coloured blanket. The saloon of The Patchwork Snail was deliciously warm and entirely lit by fairy lights. The flames from the wood-burning stove sent dancing shadows across the walls and the gentle creaking and sighing of the boat in the chilly canal made a comforting background to their conversation.

Rita had just had a bath. She was wearing her pink kimono with a red bath towel round her head. She still had her earrings on and they added to the sparkle of the surroundings. 'Honeybunch,' she said giving Honeysuckle a hug, 'I think you and your Dog Walkers are blooming brilliant!' Honeysuckle grinned.

Rita continued. 'Look how many clients you've got now and how grateful they all are – giving you cheques and presents all over the place! It's fantastic!'

Honeysuckle felt her tummy flip with excitement. She had enough money now to buy her friends Christmas presents and something really special for her mum – she would go shopping the next day and see what treasures she could find. 'I suppose none of this would have happened,' she said, brushing the crumbs from one of Mrs Whitely-Grub's mince pies off her lap, 'if Sergeant Mo—' (She stopped herself just in time from saying Motormouth.) 'If Sergeant Monmouth hadn't told us all those awful stories . . .'

'Hmm,' said Rita and then, turning to face Honeysuckle she added, 'I think Sergeant Monmouth talks a lot of old twaddle . . .' Honeysuckle saw her mum's eyes twinkle.

'He does talk a lot,' she agreed.

Rita began to laugh. 'He certainly does,' she said, giggling. 'On and on and on . . .'

Just then, they felt The Patchwork Snail begin to sway and shudder as heavy police boots stepped on to the deck. 'I tell you what,' whispered Rita, 'let's batten down the hatches, be as quiet as a couple of ghosts and pretend that we're not here . . . then perhaps he'll go away and leave us in peace!'

'OK!' Honeysuckle whispered back. She smiled to herself in the twinkling warmth inside the houseboat, while the dark, frosty air outside sprinkled glitter over the moonlit, icy water. Honeysuckle Sabrina Florette Lovelace was certain that for all her fortune-telling powers she didn't need to look in her crystal ball to know that this was going to be the best Christmas ever.

Cherry Whytock

Honeysuckle Lovelace

The Dog Walkers' Club

There comes a time in almost everybody's life when
they have a brilliant idea. Honeysuckle Lovelace's
Brilliant Idea is to set up a Dog Walkers' Club with
her friends. She can spend time with her favourite
animals *and* earn some money to help mend the leaky
houseboat where she and her mum live.

The club's first 'client' is Cupid, Mrs Whitely-Grub's
pinky-white poodle, who barely even passes for a dog.
As Cupid becomes a regular client, Honeysuckle is
increasingly suspicious of his owner. She's determined
to solve the mysteries surrounding Mrs Whitely-Grub
– and the Dog Walkers' Club provides the perfect cover!

www.piccadillypress.co.uk

☆ The latest news on forthcoming books

☆ Chapter previews

☆ Author biographies

☆ Fun quizzes

☆ Reader reviews

☆ Competitions and fab prizes

☆ Book features and cool downloads

☆ And much, much more . . .

Log on and check it out!

Piccadilly Press